The Curious Adventures of Sherlock Holmes in Japan

Dale Furutani

D1236091

Miharu Publishing

MiharuPublishing@aol.com

Printed in the United States of America

Dedication

For the next generation in Japan: Marie, Kaho, Maki, Erika, Mayuka, Yukito, Nanaka, and Wataru

Acknowledgements

I would like to thank Masae Yamamoto and Misa Arai for their invaluable help in doing research in Japan for this book. I would also like to thank Mr. Tsutomu Tomita, Chief Planner of the Mampei Hotel, Karuizawa, Japan; the staff of the National Diet Museum in Tokyo; the staff of the Shinagawa Rekishikan Museum; Shigeki and Eiko Miyamoto, and numerous others who helped me. I would also like to acknowledge the loving support of my wife Sharon and my second mother, Rosemarie Ireland Short.

Contents

Author's Foreword

"I'm so glad I found someone to give this to before I died." Tears started flowing down the *obaasan's* face.

I was embarrassed.

"Are you sure there isn't someone else you can give this to?"

The old woman shook her head. "No, no. There's no one. Besides, you are the perfect person to get this." She lifted the small wooden chest and handed it to me.

Instinctively, I leaned forward and took the chest out of her hands. My intention was to relieve her of the burden of lifting the chest but she took it as a gesture of acceptance. She sat back, sighed contentedly, and smiled. I thought it would be churlish of me to continue refusing the gift, although the Japanese way would be to refuse at least a few more times before graciously accepting.

I looked at the box, curious about it. It was carved in the Karuizawa-bori style, the distinct type of carving done in the Karuizawa area. The top had a neat border of deeply incised cherry blossoms marching around it, done in a rustic style and painted a delicate pink with hints of red. Most Karuizawa-bori carving involves flowers of some type, so that was not unusual. What was unusual was the weight of the box. There was obviously something in it.

"Can I open it?" I asked.

"*Douzo*. Please…" the obaasan said. I knew her name but couldn't help thinking of her as "obaasan," or grandmother, even though she was no direct relation to me. She was too elderly to be thought of as an *obasan*, or "aunty," and too cheerful and friendly to be thought of with some more formal title.

I lifted the lid and looked inside. There was a stack of notebooks. Some had leather covers and a few had cloth covers. I reached inside and pulled out the top one. When I opened it I saw the slightly yellowed pages were covered with a combination of Japanese kanji and English writing, written in a fading ink. The English looked like dialog, with a few kanji characters interspersed with the English words. The rest of the writing was done in a precise kanji that indicated an ordered mind. I had no idea what the notebook was.

"Are you sure you want to give these to me?" I asked again.

"You are a Furutani and Nao-chan told me you are a writer. That's all I needed to know. You are the perfect person to have them. You will know what to do with them."

She said the last with absolute conviction, although I had no idea what I was going to do with this present. Still, the box was beautiful and even if its contents proved useless the box alone was a wonderful gift, especially to a stranger. I thanked the woman lavishly and we commenced to finish our tea.

On the train ride back to Tokyo from Karuizawa I looked at the notebooks in more detail. They were primarily in kanji so I couldn't understand what they said. My Japanese is, at best, infantile. The sections written in English were usually long snatches of dialog, apparently transcribed from memory. Throughout the notebooks I kept seeing the name Sigerson-san, written in English, which had a familiar ring to me, although I couldn't exactly place where I had heard the name before.

Whatever they were, I was intrigued enough by the notebooks to enlist the aid of Japanese friends to decipher the Meiji-era Japanese found within their covers. After receiving some preliminary reports about their contents, I became very excited about the notebooks.

I thought initially that the notebooks might be fiction, written in a strange polyglot of Japanese and English. I soon understood that the notebooks were more like detailed notes of the author's observations and adventures with Sigerson-san. The notebooks were in the nature of case notes, much like a doctor might make about a patient. Since the author of the notebooks was a doctor, Dr. Junichi Watanabe, this is entirely understandable.

What got me excited, however, was I remembered where I heard the name Sigerson before. In the Sherlock Holmes story, *The Adventure of the Empty House*, Holmes tells Watson, "You may have read of the remarkable explorations of a Norwegian named Sigerson, but I am sure that it never occurred to you that you were receiving news of your friend."

Sigerson was the alias used by Sherlock Holmes when he was out of England, hiding from Professor Moriarty's gang after the incident at the Reichenbach Falls, where Holmes faked his death. Holmes admitted to visiting Tibet in the story but I had no idea he also visited Japan.

The fact that he came to Japan became obvious, however, when I reread *The Adventure of the Empty House*. Later in the story Holmes said, "I have some knowledge, however, of *baritsu*, or the Japanese system of wrestling, which has more than once been very useful to me."

London in the early 1890s was not replete with *doujou* (Japanese martial arts practice halls). Although Japanese culture enjoyed a faddish popularity in Victorian England, the timing of *The Adventure of the Empty House* means that the only place Holmes could have learned a Japanese martial art was Japan. Baritsu, which I believe is a variant of jujitsu, was introduced to London in 1899, many years after Holmes's statement in *The Adventure of the Empty House*. I had historical proof, in the original Holmes stories, that indicated that Holmes was in Japan!

I actually shook with excitement at the possibilities inherent in these notebooks. They chronicled a heretofore unknown part of the great detective's life: His time in Japan.

I haven't waited for all the notebooks to be translated. Interpreting the notes can be a laborious process because the Japanese is a bit archaic and some of the passages are cryptic. I had my friends sort the notebooks in chronological order and this book is based on the first notebook's contents.

The notes by Dr. Watanabe have considerable detail and large snatches of dialogue, but they were not actually written as stories. In some places I've had to interpret the meaning of the notes, based on research on Japan during 1892-1893, the period when Holmes must have been in Japan. I hope the spirit of Dr. Watanabe forgives me for any errors I've introduced.

I don't know much about Dr. Junichi Watanabe's life. Any reader interested in what I have been able to find out or in learning more about how I got his notebooks can refer to the Author's End Note.

Although I have written the stories as if Dr. Watanabe had written them, the voice in the stories is my own. The events of the stories, however, are true and follow as faithfully as possible the observations, thoughts, and musings that Dr. Watanabe recorded over a century ago.

The Adventure of the Henna Gaijin

A strange stranger comes

and enters my humble home.

Adventure begins.

Some Japanese think that all *gaijin* are *henna gaijin*. Of course, every foreigner is different but not all of them are "weird foreigners." Still, it's hard to dispute that some of the gaijin who come to Japan are genuinely strange.

In my experience, the most unusual henna gaijin I've met was also the most brilliant. He was a Norwegian called Sigerson-san. He was by turns perceptive and blind; sensitive and numb; refined and boorish; brilliant and hopelessly ignorant, at least about Japan. Despite sharing many adventures with this man, he was almost as much a cipher the last time I saw him as the first time I met him: Truly a henna gaijin.

Before continuing, I suppose I should tell you a little bit about myself so you can see if I am a good judge of what is weird in a foreigner.

My name is Junichi Watanabe. I am a Japanese physician who specializes in Dutch Medicine. To advance my knowledge of Dutch Medicine I studied for over two years in London, England, before returning to Japan in 1889.

I know it's unusual to study Dutch Medicine in England instead of Germany but I had many reasons for doing so. First, my ancestors are from the Satsuma clan. As you may know, individuals from Satsuma dominate the Japanese Navy and our Navy is modeled on and mentored by the English. Therefore there was a natural familiarity with English ways for me because many of my clan members knew Englishmen. Second, because of the English affinity to the Satsuma clan, I had studied the English language for many years in school. I had also studied German, of course, because of my interest in science. German is, after all, now the language of science. However I was much more comfortable reading and speaking English. Third, perhaps unreasonably, I thought that as an island nation like Japan, the English might have a better understanding of our circumstances than the Germans, who are a land power. Finally, as was famously reported in the Japanese press, the German doctors Hilgendorf and Wernich, who taught medicine in Japan, said it was "impossible" to make efficient medical practitioners of Japanese. Like many Japanese I was insulted by this evaluation from two men we had welcomed into our country and I was not eager to study in Germany when the German doctors in Japan expressed such contempt and bias towards our medical abilities.

So I went to England to study and I received a thorough education in both Dutch Medicine and what it was like for me to be the "gaijin" in the land of the gaijin.

When I returned to Japan I realized there were many physicians of Dutch Medicine in Tokyo and Yokohama. Chinese Medicine, of course, is much more popular here in Japan but the competition in the field of Dutch Medicine is still quite intense around the Capital, even though most of the physicians practicing Dutch Medicine have not studied in Europe. Therefore I resolved to find a place to start my medical practice where the competition was not so stiff and where the populace might be open to Dutch Medicine.

As you might know, the city of Karuizawa is a very popular retreat for the English and Canadian expatriates living in Japan. It is located in the mountains north of Tokyo, along the old Nakasendo Road. It was a welcome stopping point for travelers on the Nakasendo for centuries, but in recent days travel along the old road has dropped to a trickle as the railroad has been introduced to Japan and a new highway bypassed the town. Karuizawa's former glory faded.

Despite the drop in road traffic, Karuizawa still enjoys an enviable topography and climate. With its crisp mountain air and beautiful surroundings, it's a refreshing escape from the crowding and oppressive heat and humidity of a Tokyo summer. This quality was recognized by an Anglican Church missionary, Archdeacon A. C. Shaw, who built a cabin in Karuizawa about 15 years ago. Shaw told others about Karuizawa and his proselytizing for the area must have been no less fervent that his preaching for the Christian God, for he successfully got many other gaijin to follow him to Karuizawa. In the 15 years since Shaw built his cabin, Karuizawa has become revitalized as a gaijin summer community. Recently the new *Usui Shin Tetsudo* railroad became operational and the city is less than a day's journey from Tokyo, adding to its popularity.

There is a small year-round community of gaijin living in Karuizawa, but the summer is when the expatriate community swells by ten-fold. Since I acquired an excellent knowledge of the English language from my time in England I endeavored to see how this could be used and the city of Karuizawa, with its English and Canadian population, seemed like a natural place to start my practice. I would, of course, treat Japanese as part of my practice but I hoped the bulk of my income would come from the gaijin who live in or visit Karuizawa. Thus I went to Karuizawa and started practicing medicine. Over the past few years I have experienced both great joy and great sadness there.

Quite unexpectedly, one day in 1892, my surgery was visited by the Englishman, Col. Montague Ashworth. Col. Ashworth was a patient of mine, at least when he spent time in Karuizawa instead of Tokyo. I believe he was attached to the British Legation in some capacity although it was not totally clear what his duties were. In any case, he was not one of those gaijin hired by our government to advise us on the current modernization of our navy, army, and industry.

Col. Ashworth is an imposing man, tall and with a sturdy build. He was 55 at the time of our talk, still retaining a military set to his spine but supporting a slowly ballooning belly that, if he was not careful, in a few years might require serious alterations to all his jackets and waistcoats. He was normally in robust health and quite vigorous in all his actions and endeavors, however, and had only seen me for minor ailments such as a cold or two.

Like many Europeans, he sported a full mustache and beard. In his younger days his hair was that strange yellow color, but now it was mostly white. His eyes were of that pale gray that some gaijin have and his face was weather-beaten and creased from many days campaigning in the field as an officer in the British army.

I was a bit surprised when Col. Ashworth informed me that his visit was somewhat social and not because he was seeking a medical consultation. Being informed of this, I invited Col. Ashworth to my parlor instead of my consulting room.

I should mention that my practice, like that of most doctors, is in my house. I constructed this house partially based on Western principles instead of in the traditional Japanese fashion. The downstairs holds my surgery and waiting room, a parlor, dining room, and the kitchen. Upstairs the house is more traditionally Japanese, with *shouji* screens and *tatami* rooms. Behind the house is another small structure that houses the large wooden *ofuro* bathtub.

As we settled into the parlor I had Hosokawa-san, my housekeeper, bring us tea. I requested *koucha*, black tea, instead of the more common *ocha*, green tea. The koucha was, of course, served in a Western style tea service and the Colonel and I sat there pinching the handles of white teacups between our thumb and forefinger as we talked.

"How can I assist you, Colonel?" I asked.

"You can help me by taking in a boarder, albeit a temporary one."

"A boarder?" I was totally nonplussed.

"Yes. I'm sorry to surprise you with this request but I have received very short notice about this situation myself, so please excuse me. I have known you for a few years now, Doctor Watanabe, and I have observed you to be a man of honor and discretion."

"Thank you, Colonel. That is very kind of you to say that."

"I sincerely mean it or else I would not be asking this now. In addition to your good character, I have noticed in your remarks a certain affection for England."

"Yes. That is true. I love Japan above all other countries, of course, but I felt that I was treated decently in England when I studied there and good treatment cannot help but cause respect and affection to grow."

"Good. That is exactly what I wished to hear. Before I proceed, can I count on your discretion in keeping what I tell you confidential, even if you decide not to grant my request?"

"Of course."

"Excellent. Have you ever heard of the Norwegian explorer Sigerson?"

"Sigerson? Sigerson." I contemplated this name for a few moments and said, "I believe I have. I think I read a small piece in *The Japan Times* that a Sigerson-san was spending time with the head lama at Lhasa."

"The very same man. However, I received a communication yesterday that instead of staying in Tibet Sigerson will, in fact, be landing in Yokohama in a few days, traveling as supercargo on a British freighter. He intends to leave the vessel and spend some time in Japan. Unlike his visits to Persia and Tibet, Sigerson is interested in making his visit to Japan away from the glare of the press. That is why he left the impression he is still in Lhasa when he left the subcontinent."

"Why?"

Colonel Ashworth paused. Then, convinced I suppose that "in for a penny, in for a pound," as the English like to say, he told me more of the story of Sigerson-san.

"Apparently Sigerson has made powerful enemies in Europe. These enemies are so powerful that they may, in fact, reach into Asia and kill him. That is why he has come to Japan, to flee agents of his enemies who may harm him if he remains on the subcontinent."

As you can imagine, I was taken aback by this revelation.

"The Norwegian government does not have a legation to the Court of His Majesty the Emperor Mutsuhito. However, for reasons I am not privy to, the Foreign Ministry of Her Majesty's Government wishes to extend all aid and assistance to Sigerson. In fact, it was my government that helped Sigerson slip away unnoticed from the Indian subcontinent on a British ship. They have instructed me to find someplace in Japan where Sigerson can reside in a safe and comfortable manner and where he would not come to the attention of the press.

"I thought Karuizawa would be a good place for Sigerson to pass his time in Japan. Moreover, I think your home would be the perfect place for him to stay when in Karuizawa. My government, of course, would be happy to pay a respectable rent for his lodgings and the inconvenience he would cause you."

"It is not a question of money, Colonel, but of hospitality. Surely Sigerson-san would be much more comfortable in the newly finished Mampei Hotel. It is designed and furnished in the Western fashion and the staff there is superb. He does not have to lodge in my humble home."

"I frequent the Mampei and I know it is outstanding for the Western visitor. However, the Mampei is too public a place and has too many foreign visitors. It would be difficult for Sigerson to maintain discretion staying at such an establishment."

"Perhaps Sigerson-san would be more at home in your house in Karuizawa?" I asked.

"I thought of that, but as someone attached to the British Legation my house would draw as much attention as the Mampei."

"But he may not be comfortable in my humble house."

"Far from being humble, your house is spacious and it even has a Western style parlor where Sigerson would be quite happy, I'm sure. You have frequent contact with foreign patients and it would not cause any undue speculation if you simply introduced Sigerson as a patient under your care who is stopping for a time in Karuizawa to recover from an illness. Sigerson, of course, is not ill, but his taking exercise by hiking in the surrounding mountains would be perfectly natural if he was recovering from some illness. All in all, I believe staying at your house would be a much better solution than having him stay at the Mampei or my house."

I sucked air between my teeth, a habit that, although common in Japan, I had tried to break during my time in Europe because it is viewed as strange there. While in Europe I was successful but when confronted with the unusual situation presented by the Colonel, I reverted to this Japanese expression of hesitation.

I was reticent on many counts. I had reason to value my solitude and I was not used to having guests staying at my home. Moreover, as Japanese who have come in contact with Europeans will attest to, Europeans can be inconvenient. For instance, they often smell.

In Japan almost everyone will seek the comforts of a hot *ofuro* daily. If they are poor it may be the neighborhood public bath. If they are in better circumstances they will have their own bath. But regardless of class, personal cleanliness is an important goal, just as cleanliness is emphasized in our religious beliefs.

This is not the case in Europe. Even the better classes in Europe do not bathe every day. They usually do not engage in much manual exertion, except when hunting or participating in sports. Still, instead of bathing, the upper classes will douse themselves in various smelly perfumes, colognes, and eau de toilette. This is true even for the men. The lower classes simply do not bathe, at least on any reasonable schedule. Part of this is due to poverty (public baths for a cheap price are not widely available even in the capital city of London) and part is caused by the peculiar belief among some in the lower classes that bathing can be harmful to your health.

Consequently, a typical European will smell.

Even fresh from a bath, some Japanese think a European will have an odor from all the meat and dairy they eat. Some Japanese claim this is the smell of butter, which is why we say "*bataa kusai*," meaning something with a Western taint stinks of butter. As a man of science who has lived in Europe, I do not subscribe to this belief. When a European has as much enthusiasm for bathing as a Japanese, he does not smell. It's just that so few of them do have this enthusiasm for cleanliness.

Col. Ashworth, for instance, has been in Japan for several years and, with a diplomat's sensitivity for others, he has picked up Japanese bathing habits. Although our two chairs were close together I detected no odor from him. My concern was whether Sigerson-san would also be as dedicated to bathing as the Colonel, especially if he was used to living in rough circumstances on his various expeditions.

There was also the matter of who wished Sigerson-san harm. Strangely enough, it did not worry me that it might put me in danger if Sigerson-san stayed with me, but it was a situation beyond what I had encountered before and I did not know how to evaluate what it meant. I would not want to put Hosokawa-san or my patients in danger by extending hospitality to someone being hunted by unknown forces.

The fact that the British Foreign Office was interested in Sigerson-san's well-being was a positive one. Britain, after all, is Japan's ally and it has helped us in many areas, such as with the adoption of Western architecture, the expansion of our railroad networks, and the growth of our navy. Still, I wondered what inviting Sigerson-san into my house would mean from a practical standpoint.

"I see you are a bit apprehensive," Col. Ashworth said to me.

"Candidly, I am hesitant. It is an unusual request under unusual circumstances."

"I understand completely. Why don't I propose the following? I will bring Sigerson to Karuizawa the day after he arrives in Yokohama and let's have a nice tea together. I have not discussed this proposal with him so he, too, may have some hesitancy. Unless both of you agree to the arrangement, Sigerson can stay at the Mampei for the night and return to Tokyo the next day. At worst Sigerson will have a pleasant diversion in Karuizawa and you will have a chance to meet a well-known explorer. At best you two may hit it off and Sigerson will have found a wonderful place to stay while he is in Japan."

"Agreed," I said.

Thus a few days later I was waiting for the afternoon train from Tokyo in the square fronting the Karuizawa train station.

My time in London made me appreciative of small Japanese cities like Karuizawa. If you lived in a European city you would not be aware of the things that make a hamlet like Karuizawa charming. For instance, it goes without saying that the streets are clean in Karuizawa. Every shop owner and household knows that it is part of their duties to sweep and maintain the area in front of their building. To some extent this is true of the richer parts of London, but the poorer parts of that city take no pride in cleaning the street. Night soil, garbage and other foul material is often dumped in the street with no concern for neighbors or passers-by.

Another noticeable difference between Japan and a European city is the use of natural wood and the style of our buildings. The European will often paint his wood and the roofs may be made of a hodge-podge of materials, not just the tile or thatch found on our buildings. Our buildings are made to live with nature, with large screens or panels that slide open to invite nature into the home or shop, but in London the walls are most definitely made to keep nature out.

Public buildings in London are very ornate. Here a building modeled on the Chinese style can also be ornate, but the natural Japanese style is very pure and simple. For instance, we will often use natural tree limbs to act as beams or posts in our buildings, retaining their original shapes and harmonizing them into the structure of the building. We will not hack and saw the wood to conform to some arbitrary geometric shape. This reflects our love of nature.

All these elements could be found in the buildings ringing the station square at Karuizawa and I stood looking about me and enjoying them. Of course, other people occupied the square. There were several mendicant priests in the square, with their black robes, round straw hats partially covering their faces, wooden walking staves with the metal rings on top that announced their presence with a pleasant jingle, and wooden begging bowls. There were a few *jinrikisha*, that European invention, standing by to pick up people alighting from the train who did not wish to walk to their destinations in town, as well as men with handcarts to haul luggage. A few shoppers were also in the square, buying staples or looking at the *omiyage* that were found in the souvenir shops that lined the square. I sometimes think that half the Japanese economy is based on omiyage, the obligatory gifts we have to bring back to neighbors, friends and coworkers when we visit any place outside of our city.

I checked my pocket watch and, as I did so, I heard the squeal of the whistle from the *Usui Shin Tetsudo* train. It was right on time. In a few minutes the train pulled into the station with a chugging sound and large puffs of steam, finally coming to a jolting halt.

As usual with a train arrival, there were a few moments of confused activity. The excess steam from the engine swirled about the platform, looking very much like the thick fog in the city of London. The passengers gathered their belongings and exited the train and porters rushed to gather the heavier luggage. People were greeted by friends and relatives and the station, which was a silent haven a few minutes before, was now filled with a cacophony of voices. Several gaijin were on the train (something not unusual for Karuizawa), but I was able to immediately pick out Col. Ashworth and a tall companion as they exited a first class carriage. A mendicant priest approached the two men. Col. Ashworth absently reached in his pocket for a few coins as he scanned the platform looking for me. The entire scene was like countless other train arrivals I had seen but there was something slightly odd about this particular arrival, although I couldn't quite put my finger on what it was.

Perhaps it was the appearance of Sigerson-san. I had never met a Norwegian during my stay in London so I didn't know quite what to expect. The man next to Col. Ashworth was tall and thin to the point of gauntness. Of course he had been traveling a great deal in rough country and the stress of hard travel tends to make people lose weight. From Sigerson-san's appearance I thought Col. Ashworth's suggested story about Sigerson-san needing to recuperate in Karuizawa to improve his health might actually be more truth than lie.

Sigerson-san was wearing a tweed suit of sturdy cloth and sensible traveling shoes. Around his shoulders was a traveling cape and on his head was the type of cap the English call a "deerstalker." All in all this was a sensible traveling outfit for a European, but somehow I expected something a little more exotic from a Norwegian and not something so typically English.

Sigerson-san's face was also English. Some Japanese say the gaijin faces are all alike, with bushy hair and enormous noses. However, in London, in addition to English, I met Germans, French and Italians and learned that gaijin faces can fall into patterns that even the Europeans describe as "typical" for a particular nationality. With his narrow oval face and large nose that the English call "Roman," I would consider Sigerson-san's face as typical of the English upper class.

Sigerson-san's eyes were his most striking feature. Falconry and hawking are still popular sports in mountainous regions like Karuizawa so I've had occasion to see predatory birds up close. Sigerson-san's eyes were exactly like those feathered hunters. They were dark, clear and intense. He was looking about him on the platform with an intent gaze, not like the wide-eyed wonderment you often see with new visitors to Japan. His observations seemed to have a purpose, as if he were a student intently examining a particularly important book.

As I approached him and Col. Ashworth, Sigerson-san fixed his gaze on me. I admit it was an uncomfortable feeling. We Japanese are reluctant to stare into the eyes of strangers because we feel it might be rude. Europeans have no such inhibitions and, indeed, I learned they may view you with suspicion if you don't look them in the eyes. Sigerson-san did more than look at my eyes. He looked at me from head to toe, then stared at me as though his gaze were drilling through me. He did this quickly and methodically and it made me feel much like a specimen instead of a person. I was not sure I liked Sigerson-san at this point.

"My dear Dr. Watanabe," the Colonel said to me. As a diplomat, he had learned to bow instead of shaking hands but, as with most gaijin, he didn't understand the subtleties of how deeply you bow and how stiff you hold your back, depending on the perceived social rank of the person you are bowing to. I wish gaijin would just stop trying to bow and simply shake hands.

"I want to introduce you to Sigerson," the Colonel continued. "Sigerson, this is Dr. Watanabe." As if he were reading my mind, Sigerson-san did not ape a bow and instead he extended his hand. It was a thin hand with long fingers and he shook my hand in a quick and not overly-firm manner.

"Gentlemen, it is a great pleasure to welcome you to Karuizawa. I trust the trip from Tokyo was pleasant," I said.

"Yes," the Colonel answered, "the completion of the rail line to Tokyo makes the journey to Karuizawa most convenient."

"Good. Gentlemen, if you don't mind I thought we could go to my house for some tea. It is only a short walk from the station. Of course, Karuizawa is so compact that most things are only a short walk from the station."

Sigerson-san and the Colonel readily agreed and we made our way to my house. As we walked we made small talk, or rather the Colonel and I made small talk. Sigerson-san only spoke a few times, usually to ask about things he saw on the way that interested him. I explained that the large mountain he saw was Mount Asama, that Karuizawa had been a stopping place on the famous Nakasendo road in Japan, and that its current size and prosperity were relatively new phenomena, spurred by the Archdeacon A. C. Shaw, who started promoting it as a summer spot for gaijin.

Sigerson-san asked his questions in English that seemed perfect, causing me embarrassment that a Norwegian could master this difficult language when I, despite living there and studying diligently, still had an accent and many gaps in my knowledge of the tongue.

When we finally reached my house Sigerson-san seemed surprised when the Colonel and I took our shoes off in the entryway. "It's a tradition here in Japan to help keep the house clean and to prevent undue wear on tatami mats, which are the floor coverings in many Japanese homes," I explained. "They don't follow this custom in some Western establishments like the Mampei Hotel and I don't ask my foreign patients to do this when they visit my surgery, but in a private home, even decorated in the Western style like mine, it is something that is expected."

"Of course," Sigerson-san said, and he promptly took off his shoes.

We settled in the parlor and Hosokawa-san came to see if we wanted our tea. Hosokawa-san has been the maid in my house since it was built. She is an older woman who was widowed a few years back and became a maid to support herself. She is a bit plump, so she is unusual among Japanese women of her age, who are usually quite slight. She can have the gruff manner of country people raised in the mountains but she helped me through a difficult time and has a very good heart. As a result she can sometimes take the kind of liberties a servant who has been with a family for decades will do, but I understand she has my best interest in mind and therefore pretend I don't notice her ways of expression.

I saw one such quirk from her when she served the tea. She had gone to town to buy scones from the English baker (who is really Japanese) and now these scones were on the tray with the tea. However, instead of clotted cream, which is admittedly difficult to find in Karuizawa, on the tray was a serving of marmalade and an absurdly large tub of butter. I looked at Hosokawa and she wrinkled her nose at me, as if she smelled something unpleasant.

If the Colonel understood the jibe represented by the butter he was diplomatic enough not to comment on it. Instead, he acted as "mother" and offered to pour the tea for us.

As we settled back with our tea and scones, Sigerson-san looked at me and said, "I hope you enjoyed studying at Victoria Hospital in London, Doctor Watanabe, and that you don't miss the exercise of rowing too much."

The Colonel knew I studied in London but I didn't recall ever telling him where.

"How did you know that, Sigerson?" the Colonel asked, echoing my thoughts exactly. His voice also echoed the surprise that I felt.

"On the Doctor's watch chain is a small seal of The City. It must have special meaning to him because he carries it constantly, and therefore it was not obtained as part of a casual visit to London. You told me he specializes in Western style medicine, what you say the Japanese call Dutch Medicine, so it was a natural deduction that his time spent in London was for studying his specialty. Of the hospitals in London, Victoria is known for many foreign students, so it was easy to deduce that Victoria was the hospital he studied at."

"And the rowing?" the Colonel asked.

"The Doctor has some small calluses on his hands. As a physician it is obvious he didn't get them through the course of his occupation, so it must have been through some sport or hobby. If you look at the position of the calluses it is easy to see they came from manipulating oars. Moreover, the calluses are old and have softened over time, which means that Dr. Watanabe has not been rowing recently."

"My goodness, Sigerson, that is a surprising parlor trick. But now that you've explained it I can see it's perfectly simple and not as amazing as I first thought it was," the Colonel said.

Sigerson-san shot the Colonel a glance. It was plain he was annoyed at the Colonel's characterization of his observations and deductions as a simple parlor trick.

"I don't mean to disagree, Colonel," I said, "but I think Sigerson-san's powers of observation and his ability to draw conclusions from them are amazing." Sigerson-san flashed a brief smile. It flitted across his face so quickly that it would have been missed if one looked away for a moment. This allowed me to make some observations and deductions of my own: Sigerson-san had an ego to match his agile mental abilities and was pleased when someone appreciated his powers.

"I don't want to violate any Japanese customs I might not know about, Dr. Watanabe, but I would like to extend my condolences over the loss of your beloved wife."

Col. Ashworth exploded with surprise. "How the deuce do you know that?" he asked, his shock at Sigerson-san's statement making him forget his usual diplomatic language. He looked at me. "Is that true, Dr. Watanabe? Have you lost a wife?"

"Yes," I stammered. We Japanese are taught to try and maintain an even demeanor when dealing with others. Westerners claim this makes us "inscrutable" but this is only because they cannot discern the subtle facial expressions we make or the nuances of our gestures and language. In this instance, however, my reaction was not at all subtle. I was astounded at Sigerson-san's statement and showed it. I could not understand how he could know this. My wife had died within a year of our marriage, soon after we moved to Karuizawa. Most of my gaijin patients, including Col. Ashworth, made my acquaintance after her death. Only Hosokawa-san and a few other residents of Karuizawa knew of my personal tragedy.

"I am sorry if I upset you," Sigerson-san said with apparent sincerity. "It was my intention only to pass on my regret at your loss."

"But how did you know this?" Col. Ashworth asked again.

"It was perfectly simple and elementary," Sigerson-san said. "No explanation should be necessary for a mere parlor trick."

Col. Ashworth stared at Sigerson-san open mouthed. Then he said, "All right, I deserved that," he conceded. "Your ability is no parlor trick. Please tell me how you know about Dr. Watanabe's late wife and I promise to not make an ass of myself by dismissing your methods."

Sigerson-san hesitated a second, savoring his victory, then he said, "If you look at this parlor you will see that there is a certain delicacy and, dare I say it, femininity to this room. The small flowers on the wallpaper, the placement of slender vases, and the choices of color all bespeak a woman's touch, and a young and vibrant woman at that. Some men may also be capable of this delicacy of feeling, especially since I am not familiar with Japanese culture, but when I look at Dr. Watanabe I see a man who is interested in sports like rowing, not the selection of wallpaper. Despite this obvious womanly influence, the only woman we have been introduced to is the maid. Dr. Watanabe is a proper gentleman and yet he did not introduce us to a wife or mother, so she must not be a resident at this time."

"But how did you know it was his wife and how did you know she is deceased?" Ashworth asked.

"The waiting room and surgery is the Doctor's business domain and visitors there, especially foreign visitors, may wear shoes. The rest of the house was the domain of another and she preferred the Japanese custom of removing one's shoes. Although the custom of keeping shoes on could easily have been extended to this Western style parlor, it has not, indicating that Dr. Watanabe has wanted to preserve this lady's preferences even though she is not here. That shows a certain tenderness and sensitivity. Finally, although Dr. Watanabe is of an age when, I suppose, most men would be married in Japan. He is not, which indicates that he might have been once married but he is not married now. Combine this with the tender concern for the wishes of a younger woman who is not here and you come to the conclusion that, sadly, the Doctor's wife has passed."

Col. Ashworth looked at me and said, "Is that true?"

"Yes."

"Amazing," the Colonel said.

It was at that moment that I decided that Sigerson-san would be a most interesting house- guest.

We Japanese tend to lead ordered lives. That may be why we crave novelty. We are captured by fads of the moment, like the frenzy over Western style dancing a decade ago caused by the dances at the *Rokumeikan* building in Tokyo. That is why we love to travel to new places. That may be why we are adventurous with foods that Westerners consider strange. That is why I decided to invite Sigerson-san into my home. He was the most unusual and interesting gaijin I have met, either in Japan or Europe. In short, he was the most exotic of novelties; an interesting henna gaijin.

The details of Sigerson-san's stay were soon settled and Hosokawa-san was asked to send someone to the station to pick up Sigerson-san's luggage, which turned out to be a single bag, suitable for a man traveling fast and light and sometimes in rough country. In less than an hour I was showing Sigerson-san the room he would stay in.

When he saw the room he said the obvious. "There is no furniture."

"In Japan we sit on the floor and we sleep on lightly padded mats called *futon*. During the day the futon and the rest of your bedding will be folded up and put away in a closet by Hosokawa-san. In the evening Hosokawa-san will remove the futon and bedding and lay them out in your room. She will also set a candle or lamp in the room, if you wish, but I think you will find the parlor more comfortable until it is time for you to retire."

I dare say that most Japanese have not seen a gaijin in person and even fewer have actually had a gaijin in their house. While we try to study European customs when we travel there, gaijin seem blissfully unaware of Japanese customs. They sometimes ignore our customs even when they know them.

Following his lead in deduction I observed that Sigerson-san wore no wedding ring so he was not married. He was neat, but it was obvious that Sigerson-san was used to the rough life of an explorer. His sturdy shoes were worn and his suit, although it was clean and presentable, was hard used. He sprawled in his seat and it didn't take his deductive powers to realize that even when he was in the relative comforts of Western civilization he probably led the rather sloppy life of a bachelor. This caused conflict when Sigerson-san returned from taking a short walk before dinner.

Sigerson-san forgot to take his shoes off when he entered the parlor.

When Sigerson-san entered the parlor I was sitting at a table doing some paperwork associated with my practice. Sigerson-san entered and flopped down on the settee, his shoes prominently displayed. I was deciding how to diplomatically bring up the subject of his shoes when Hosokawa-san appeared at the parlor door, perhaps to announce that dinner would soon be ready. Hosokawa-san, of course, immediately fixed her eyes on Sigerson-san's feet. Her eyes narrowed in surprise and anger.

It would cause embarrassment to me if Hosokawa-san showed her displeasure by expressing her anger verbally. Therefore Hosokawa-san left without saying anything but she appeared a few moments later with a bucket and some rags. She bowed in a polite fashion then set to work scrubbing the carpet in a track that led from the door to Sigerson-san.

I was about to reprimand Hosokawa-san for her rudeness but Sigerson-san immediately removed his shoes and carried them into the hallway. "I do apologize," he said to me.

"It's nothing," I said, even though I was unreasonably upset by his breach of etiquette.

"But it is something that I should have remembered. Does your housekeeper speak English?"

"Only a few words like hello or thank you. Many people in Karuizawa have a limited knowledge of English because of the British population here, but only a few are fluent and they usually work at the hotel or in some of the shops."

"Then will you translate for me?"

"Of course."

"What is your housekeeper's name?"

"Hosokawa-san." At the sound of her name Hosokawa-san stopped scrubbing.

"Please tell Hosokawa-san I am extremely sorry at my rudeness in keeping my shoes on. I was immersed in thought about a problem and when I am so engaged I often forget my surroundings. I had no intention of breaking a Japanese taboo. I also want to assure her, and you, too, Doctor, that I had no intention of violating the wishes of the departed lady who established the rules in this house regarding where shoes may and may not be worn. Please extend my sincere apology."

I translated this to Hosokawa-san. Sigerson-san's apology seemed to partially mollify her.

"Will he also take a bath today?" Hosokawa-san said, wrinkling her nose. She had heard of the rumors about gaijin and their bathing habits.

I decided not to reprimand Hosokawa-san because, unlike Col. Ashworth, Sigerson-san actually did have a faint odor about him. I attributed this to his long voyage and not his eating habits. "Yes, I will tactfully suggest he might want to use the ofuro after dinner. Just make sure you don't heat the tub to its normal temperature because Europeans seem unable to take Japanese-style hot water. They like to bathe in water we would consider tepid. After he is done you can add more wood and heat the water to a proper temperature."

"If I may speak frankly," Hosokawa-san said, "will you also instruct him in the proper use of the ofuro?" As a servant, Hosokawa-san would use the bath last so she was concerned that the water remained clean. Gaijin were notorious for climbing into a Japanese bath dirty instead of properly cleaning themselves before entering the bath to soak. Frankly, since I would allow Sigerson-san to use the bath first because he was the guest, and I would follow him, I was concerned about the same thing.

"Yes. I will show him the bucket, soap and cloths and instruct him on cleaning himself before he enters the bath water."

That, and the apology, seemed to mollify Hosokawa-san somewhat. She bowed to us both and asked me to assure Sigerson-san that his wearing of shoes in the parlor was quite all right, even though we both knew this was only a polite way to smooth over a social gaffe.

We ate the dinner Hosokawa-san prepared in the main room upstairs. Since the upstairs of my house is in the Japanese style, unlike the ground floor, which is in the Western style, we ate sitting on *zabuton* cushions, sitting on the tatami. Sigerson-san seemed to have trouble placing his long Western legs because they would not fit under the low table the food was on, but he managed to position himself like a Western lady riding side-saddle on a horse, with his legs stretched out parallel to the table. If he found the

Japanese fare not to his liking he had the good sense to keep it to himself. Instead he ate everything presented to him and, after eating an astounding four bowls of rice, Sigerson-san asked me to compliment Hosokawa-san on the cooking.

Thus the first "crisis" with Sigerson-san staying at my house was smoothed over, although I knew Hosokawa-san was still not very satisfied with the arrangement. I know this because, despite the fact she had prepared a Japanese style dinner, Hosokawa-san placed another huge container of butter in front of Sigerson-san.

The next morning I was reading the *Karuizawa Shimbun* newspaper when Sigerson-san joined me for breakfast. I had instructed Hosokawa-san to make a Western style breakfast of toast, koucha, and *onsen* eggs (eggs boiled in the shell, just like they do at hot springs), instead of the typical Japanese breakfast of rice, miso soup and grilled fish.

"Good morning, Sigerson-san," I said. "I trust you slept well."

"Actually I am a bit stiff because the futon is so lightly padded, but it was still much more pleasant than sleeping in the wild or a tossing bunk on a ship. Is that the local newspaper?" he asked.

"Yes. Unfortunately there was a terrible crime here yesterday afternoon."

Sigerson-san's interest was immediately piqued. "What kind of crime?"

"Murder."

"Oh really? What are the circumstances?" I stared at Sigerson-san. I had never seen a man become so suddenly animated over a newspaper account of a crime.

"I'll roughly translate the newspaper article for you. The Abbot of Sozenji Temple in Karuizawa was found murdered yesterday when the monks returned from their daily begging. He was struck on the head in the courtyard of the temple and apparently died instantly. The neighbors near the temple did not observe anything unusual." I paused.

"That's it?"

"Yes, I'm afraid so."

Almost to himself, Sigerson-san said, "Details. Details. I must have details to know anything about this crime."

"I beg your pardon?"

He looked at me. "I'm sorry, Dr. Watanabe. It's just that criminal investigation is a kind of..." he paused for a word, "hobby. I have not engaged in it much with my travels and this case sounds interesting. Before I took to exploring I was actually a Consulting Detective."

"Consulting Detective? Consulting Detective? I understand the words but I don't quite know what this means."

"It's a new profession recently invented by a man in London. He has become quite famous for his work in the field of criminal investigation. Perhaps you have heard of him? His name is Sherlock Holmes." For some reason Sigerson-san gave me a smug smile.

I thought for a few minutes and said, "I'm afraid I'm not familiar with the name."

Sigerson-san looked crestfallen. "Well, perhaps his name has become well known since you left England. In any case, I modeled my career on his until I started traveling in the East."

I was sorry to disappoint Sigerson-san because of my lack of knowledge about his model, Sherlock Holmes. To mollify him I said, "Well, if you want, I suppose we can go visit Sozenji after my morning patients are looked at. Perhaps you can learn more about the crime there."

Sigerson-san brightened and said, "I don't suppose we can leave immediately?"

"My dear Sigerson-san," I said, "you must remember that I am a doctor, not a policeman. I must see the patients who show up at my surgery before I can help you pursue your hobby. Any decent doctor would place his priorities the same way. I would tell you how to get to Sozenji on your own but there is no guarantee that there will be anyone there who can speak English. In fact, it is most probable that the monks and neighbors do not speak English because the temple is located in the hills and not in the center of the town, where most foreigners are."

"Of course, Doctor, you are quite right. However, when you are done looking at your morning patients I would be most grateful if you could indulge me by taking me to the scene of the murder."

"It will be my pleasure," I said, although after I said it I wondered how much pleasure it could be to intrude on such a violent crime scene. However, Sigerson-san's enthusiasm for seeing the scene of the murder was infectious and, as ghoulish as it sounds, I was actually interested in going with him to see what a gaijin amateur detective would do.

Fortunately I did not have a long line of patients waiting to see me but I did spot Takada-san amongst them and my heart fell. Takada-san is a woman with a marriage-age daughter. She came to see me as a patient when I first moved to Karuizawa. Unfortunately, soon after my wife died, Takada-san started hinting that I would be a wonderful match for her daughter. Even though I was still grieving for my wife Takada-san became relentless about pushing her daughter at me until I finally had to tell her to stop. She did stop for a brief period but had lately rekindled her campaign to gain me as a son-in-law. As they say, *baka wa shinanakya naoranai*: Unless an idiot dies she won't be cured.

Fortunately, the ailments my patients had were minor but I noticed Takada-san hung back until she was the last one to see me. She entered the examination room, giving me an obsequious bow and an insincere smile.

"*Sensei!*" she greeted me a bit too heartily, rather like a Kyoto shopkeeper. "How are you?"

"I'm fine, Takada-san. More to the point, how are you? There must be something wrong for you to visit me again. I just saw you a few days ago."

"No, no, nothing is wrong, Sensei. I just wanted to tell you the medicine you gave me cured my headaches. It was wonderful of you, Sensei! To thank you, my daughter and I would like to invite you to come to our house for a nice dinner. You must miss a good home-cooked meal."

"Actually, Hosokawa-san makes me delicious meals. It's totally unnecessary to do anything extra just because a medicine I prescribed was effective. Besides, I have a house guest I must attend to. He is a Norwegian named Sigerson-san and his health requires me to stay near him, especially at mealtimes."

The last was not true, of course, but it gave me a good excuse from Mrs. Takada's dinner invitations for the duration of Sigerson-san's stay. I managed to extricate myself from Takada-san and a few minutes later Sigerson-san and I were able to start walking to the temple.

If you have not been there, then I should assure you that Karuizawa really is a lovely spot. Unlike Tokyo, where the air seems perpetually oppressive from the crowding and smoke from industry and cooking fires, the air in the mountains around Karuizawa is crisp and sweet. The trees that border the roads muffle man-made sounds and allow one to enjoy the chirping of birds, accompanied by the counterpoint of crunching dirt sounds coming from your feet.

Sigerson-san seemed to enjoy the walk to Sozenji temple, but only partially. Mostly his attention seemed focused on reaching the temple, not on enjoying the natural beauty that surrounded him. Achieving his goal seemed to be the point of his walk, not enjoying the journey. He reminded me of a racehorse straining in the starting gate and anxious to cross the finish line.

Presently we came to the gatehouse of Sozenji temple, a modest structure of aged wood and plaster. From inside the temple I could hear the sonorous chanting of many voices praying for the repose of the late Abbot. It occurred to me that this might not be the best time to visit the temple because there would be no one to talk to us. The priests would all be involved in the funeral rites for the Abbot.

My apprehensions were allayed, however, when I saw Officer Suzuki in the temple courtyard. As the local magistrate in Karuizawa, Officer Suzuki was familiar to almost everyone in the town. He was relatively new to the area. From the normal courtesy call he made to me when he assumed his duties in the area, I knew something about his background. He was originally from Tokyo and the local gossip was that his assignment to Karuizawa was not pleasing to him, but I don't know why. Regardless, I thought Suzuki-san would be the ideal person to sate Sigerson-san's curiosity about the murder.

I went to greet Officer Suzuki. I could see that Sigerson-san was impatient with the bowing and greetings Suzuki-san and I made to each other. Gaijin are so rude! I was going to impose on Suzuki-san for information to satisfy Sigerson-san's curiosity so naturally I was going to set the proper groundwork with a proper greeting. When Suzuki-san and I had finished our greetings I introduced Sigerson-san. "Sigerson-san is staying with me while he regains his health from an illness," I told Officer Suzuki.

"*Sou desu ka*? Is that so?" Suzuki-san replied.

"Could you ask the officer exactly where the murder occurred?" Sigerson-san interjected.

I did so and Officer Suzuki said, "I understood a little of what he said. What I don't understand is why he wants to know exactly where the Abbot was killed."

"He says detecting is a sort of hobby."

Officer Suzuki sighed. "I'll never understand gaijin! What kind of person would take up investigating crimes as a hobby? Anyway, please translate for me because I have no confidence in my English, despite the fact that I must use it when dealing with the gaijin in Karuizawa."

Officer Suzuki pointed. "Right here in the entry courtyard is where the Abbot died."

"Can you ask him where exactly?" Sigerson-san said.

Officer Suzuki pointed to a spot on the ground. "The Abbot's body was found right there."

I relayed this to Sigerson-san who immediately went to the spot and fell to the ground! Both Suzuki-san and I were naturally alarmed by this development. We rushed to Sigerson-san, thinking he might have been struck by a sudden malady.

"What is wrong, Sigerson-san?" I said with concern.

Sigerson-san put up his hand to indicate he was not injured. "I pray you, please don't advance any closer! There have already been too many people on this ground and it is difficult to read what transpired here." He peered at the gravel of the courtyard with intense concentration, sweeping the ground ahead of him with a relentless gaze like a dog on the scent.

"Is the gaijin sick?" Officer Suzuki asked me.

"I think he's examining the murder site," I responded.

"It's just a gravel courtyard," Officer Suzuki shrugged. "What could he see? Sensei, your houseguest is truly a henna gaijin."

Even though Officer Suzuki was a police officer, I was about to rebuke him for calling Sigerson-san a "weird foreigner." It's true he was weird, even for a gaijin, but one should maintain some semblance of politeness if one is a police officer and not say such things so openly. Before I could say anything, however, Sigerson-san got up off the gravel and dusted himself off.

"It's quite impossible," he remarked. "There has been too much tramping about, disturbing footprints and any other clues that may have been left. One thing I did notice, however, was that most of the people around the murder site were using walking sticks of some kind."

I was surprised Sigerson-san could learn that much from examining the gravel in the courtyard. "Those were probably the mendicant priests who found the body of the Abbot," I said. "They all carry a staff to announce their presence in a neighborhood. The staff has rings on the top that jangle as they walk."

"Tell me more about these priests," Sigerson-san asked.

I shrugged, not sure what there was to tell. "The priests are in training at Sozenji, which is a Soto Zen temple. They are required to go out each day to beg for food or money. It is part of their training."

Sigerson-san looked around the temple. "But this temple seems to be in very good condition. It doesn't look like it is mired in poverty. Surely the priests here do not need to beg for food or money."

"I'm sure the temple is in sound fiscal condition. However, that is not the purpose of the begging."

"Is it to teach the priests humility?"

"I'm sure it does that, also, but that is not the real purpose. The real purpose is to afford an opportunity for the person giving the food or money to acquire a kind of blessing. The begging is for the benefit of the person giving, not receiving. For that reason the priests are required to stand in different parts of the town. They cannot simply return to a place where they know people will give them alms. They announce their presence with the jangling of the metal rings on their walking staves, or sometimes they ring a bell. They are not really soliciting alms but offering a chance to people who want to give a donation to gain merit."

"That's very interesting," Sigerson-san said.

"What's the gaijin saying, Sensei?" Officer Suzuki asked. "I couldn't follow your explanation. The English was too sophisticated for me."

"He was asking me about the mendicant priests and I was explaining about why they beg," I said.

Officer Suzuki gave me a look that clearly mirrored his opinion about the ignorance of visitors to our land regarding our customs and religion. This time I tried to ignore his rudeness. I'm sure Officer Suzuki encountered many gaijin in his duties as constable of Karuizawa. But when he encountered gaijin they were either upset as victims of crime or perpetrators of disturbances. This would naturally skew one's view of foreigners.

"It's good that he learns something about Japan, I suppose," Officer Suzuki said. "But you should tell him that a murder is not a tourist attraction."

I was sure that, if he wanted to, he could probably have told Sigerson-san his opinions himself. He said his English was poor but he frequently had to interact with the foreigners in Karuizawa so it must be passable. Officer Suzuki gave a polite salute to Sigerson-san and me and he went off, I suppose to see if he could discover more about the murderer of the Abbot.

Sigerson-san seemed oblivious to Officer Suzuki leaving, his face immersed in deep thought. "The Abbot was killed by a blow to the head?" he confirmed.

"That is what the newspaper said."

"And the story in the newspaper said nothing unusual was noticed?"

"Yes."

"Can we talk to the neighbors to see if they noticed anything?"

I might have been a bit annoyed at Sigerson-san's fixation on this tragic incident, but frankly I had become intrigued by the crime and was waiting to see what was in Sigerson-san's mind. I was sure it was not mere idle curiosity that impelled him to gather information about this murder. I suppose exploring a crime is like exploring undiscovered territory. Sigerson-san was, after all, an explorer, so he would have an inclination for such things. Therefore I took Sigerson-san from the temple and we walked back on the path leading towards Karuizawa.

Sozenji was at the top of a hill with a steep path leading up to it. At the bottom of the hill the path joined a mountain road that eventually led to a cluster of houses on the outskirts of Karuizawa. As we approached these houses an obaasan popped out and started vigorously sweeping in front of her house.

"Can we talk to that woman?" Sigerson-san asked.

"Of course."

I approached the obaasan and introduced myself as a doctor.

"Sensei," the old woman exclaimed, giving me a deep bow. Although she gave me all the courtesy I could ask for she kept one eye rudely glued on Sigerson-san. Unlike most of Japan, in Karuizawa the sight of a gaijin is not at all unusual so perhaps it was Sigerson-san's height that fascinated her. Sigerson-san, like most gaijin, stared at the woman openly, but by now I knew that Sigerson-san was exercising his amazing powers of observation instead of simply being rude.

"Can you ask her if she was home on the day the Abbot was killed?" Sigerson-san said.

I did, and the woman replied, "Yes Sensei. I told the police officer and that reporter from the *Karuizawa Shimbun* that I was home and saw nothing unusual."

I told Sigerson-san this and he asked, "Can you ask her to tell you what she saw, even if she thought it was not unusual?"

When I asked the woman this she gave me a strange look but she replied, "As I said, Sensei, I just saw the things I see every day. There were a few charcoal sellers coming down the road, some of my neighbors going into town, a priest, and the peddler who sharpens knives and scissors. I had two of my knives sharpened by the peddler."

"That's very interesting," Sigerson-san said. I couldn't see what was so interesting about the woman's remarks but before I could ask him why he found them so interesting Sigerson-san said, "Please thank her for me. Tell her she was very helpful." Then he started walking off.

I gave the woman a proper thank you and I had to walk briskly to catch up with Sigerson-san. As I reached him I said, "It was lucky that old woman came out to sweep the front of her house."

"Actually, that woman is one of those souls that have too little to do except mind the business of the neighborhood. They're very useful in this kind of investigation."

"Why do you say that?"

"The front of her house has already been swept many times today. She uses sweeping as a ruse to inspect people traveling in front of her home. The sides of her home are not as immaculate, showing that an excuse for observing the road, not cleanliness, is the attraction of sweeping."

I looked over my shoulder and saw that Sigerson-san's observation was correct. The street in front of her home was immaculate, even though the sides of her house were a trifle unkempt.

"My dear Dr. Watanabe," Sigerson-san continued, "could you send a note to Officer Suzuki asking him to meet us at the train station when the Tokyo train arrives tomorrow? Please tell him I will be able to point out who killed the Abbot at that time."

Even though I had seen several examples of Sigerson-san's powers of deduction, I was not prepared for his assertion that he had solved the murder of the holy man. I stopped walking and stared after the tall gaijin. "Who killed the Abbot?" I asked.

"Yes. I don't know his name but I will be able to identify him," Sigerson-san replied.

"If you don't know his name how can you identify him to Officer Suzuki?"

"Nonetheless I will be able to point him out to Officer Suzuki tomorrow."

That's all Sigerson-san would tell me about his solution to the crime. Despite my questions he kept what the British like to call a stiff upper lip. If you have never met an Englishman I can assure you that when they enter this mode they are quite inscrutable. It was impossible to know from Sigerson-san's expression exactly what was running through his mind.

It occurred to me that Sigerson-san might use this tactic to make himself the center of attention. A sudden unveiling is a technique used by magicians around the world to inspire awe and wonder. Still, if his claim that he was now in a position to solve the Abbot's murder was true, then Sigerson-san would truly be a magician of sorts.

The next day Sigerson-san and I were at the Karuizawa train station about 15 minutes before the arrival of the Tokyo train. Officer Suzuki arrived at approximately the same time. "Good afternoon, Sensei," Officer Suzuki said to me. "Can you tell me if this gaijin really knows who murdered the Abbot?"

I sucked air past my teeth and from that gesture Officer Suzuki knew that I was totally uncomfortable with the question. He also knew that the source of my discomfort was that I did not know the answer to his inquiry. Understanding the situation, Officer Suzuki naturally stopped questioning me about it. Instead, like Sigerson-san and me, he simply waited patiently for the Tokyo train to arrive.

I tried to remember everything Sigerson-san and I did the day before but I saw nothing that would tell Sigerson-san who had killed the Abbot. It seemed impossible that he had acquired the knowledge necessary to solve this awful crime, yet he stood next to me radiating complete confidence, even though he admitted he did not know the name of the murderer. How could this be possible? Had he seen something that told him the identity of the murderer? Was there anything I said or translated for him that could give him the key to this crime? I was completely baffled. To spare total embarrassment in front of Officer Suzuki I hoped I was dealing with the coldly rational machine I identified Sigerson-san to be and not some completely delusional henna gaijin.

The town square in front of the station showed the usual bustle that accompanied the arrival of a train. Several porters were waiting with handcarts to haul luggage for the arriving passengers. There were two horse-drawn carriages from the Mampei hotel there to pick up important guests. There were jinrikisha waiting for passengers who did not wish to walk to their destination. As usual, four or five mendicant priests were standing in the Station Square, dressed in their black robes and woven wicker hats. There were perhaps a dozen shoppers in the square visiting the food and specialty shops that clustered near the station. There were also several people like us waiting for the arrival of the train, perhaps there to meet friends or relatives. And naturally there were several uniformed employees of the railroad company making final preparations before the train's arrival. How the arrival of the train would allow Sigerson-san to identify the Abbot's murderer remained a complete mystery.

Presently we heard the sharp shriek of the train whistle and within a few moments we saw the train chugging into the station, stopping at the platform with a cloud of billowing steam. Almost immediately the doors of the carriage cars opened up and a variety of *nihonjin* and gaijin passengers stepped onto the platform. Where the platform had been virtually empty a few moments before, save for employees of the railroad, there was now a confusing crowd of Japanese and foreign guests to Karuizawa milling about.

Sigerson-san pointed his finger towards the platform. "Dr. Watanabe, do you see that priest who is approaching passengers and asking for alms?"

I looked to where Sigerson-san was pointing and, in fact, there was a mendicant priest slowly walking through the crowd, asking for alms from alighting passengers.

"Yes, I do."

"Please tell Officer Suzuki that priest murdered the Abbot."

I was startled. "Are you sure?"

"I am as sure that he murdered the Abbot as I am sure that he is not actually a priest. Please kindly tell Officer Suzuki that the man dressed as a priest is the murderer. You might also tell him to be careful because that man has already proven himself to be capable of violence."

I conveyed Sigerson-san's statement to Officer Suzuki. Officer Suzuki looked at me and said, "Sensei, he can't be serious. Perhaps it's some kind of perverse gaijin joke."

"I am sure that he is entirely serious. I can't vouch for him being accurate in this case but I've already seen many examples of Sigerson-san being uncannily accurate in his observations and deductions. I don't think it would do any harm for you to detain that priest and engage in some conversation to ascertain if he is somehow involved with the Abbot's death."

Still looking doubtful, Officer Suzuki went to the platform and approached the priest whom Sigerson-san had pointed out. Officer Suzuki and the priest engaged in a few minutes of conversation. I don't know what Officer Suzuki said but quite suddenly the priest dropped his begging bowl, grabbed his staff with both hands, and swung the walking stick viciously at the Officer's head.

Officer Suzuki, of course, was trained in jujitsu and he was able to sidestep the blow to his head, grab the walking staff, and use the momentum of the priest to throw him to the ground. Naturally confusion and turmoil ensued as this fight broke out on the crowded train platform but in a few moments Officer Suzuki was able to extract some rope from his pocket that he kept for just such occasions and he was able to tie the hands of the false priest behind him.

Sigerson-san and I rushed to the platform to aid Officer Suzuki at the start of the fight but by the time we reached the scene of the action the fight was over. Officer Suzuki had everything in hand.

Sigerson-san looked at the knots holding the false priest's hands with great interest and said, "Remarkable. This is as good as, and perhaps better than any pair of metal handcuffs we have in the West."

I thought it strange that Sigerson-san would have an almost professional interest in the kind of restraints that the police in Japan use but I was much more interested in the condition of Officer Suzuki. "Are you all right, Officer?" I asked.

"Yes. As soon as I started asking him about the death of the Abbot he tried to attack me. How did Sigerson-san know that this man is involved in the Abbot's death? And how does he know that he isn't a genuine priest?"

I translated Officer Suzuki's questions to Sigerson-san.

"I knew from the first moment I arrived in Karuizawa that there was something different about this priest. I observed that none of the other mendicant priests approached anyone to gather alms, only this one. You provided the key piece of information I needed to understand this difference, Doctor. I am not familiar with Japanese religion, but when you told me the true purpose of begging was for the benefit of the person giving the alms, not the priest receiving it, it seemed logical to me that a true priest would simply stand and receive the gifts of others. He would not actively solicit donations. You'll observe that the other priests near the station are doing precisely that. They are receiving alms, not soliciting them. Therefore it is an easy deduction that this man is not an actual priest. He is, in fact, an imposter who simply takes the guise of a priest to collect money."

I translated for Officer Suzuki and asked a question of my own to Sigerson-san. "But how much money could he actually make begging?"

"It might be surprisingly lucrative," Sigerson-san said. "There was a case of a man in London who could live a comfortable middle-class life through begging. He would leave his wife and family and commute into The City each day, just like most of his neighbors. He would go to a cheap room by the river and put on rags and theatrical makeup, giving his face a terrible visage, complete with a twisted lip. It caused a minor sensation in London when his fraud was revealed by a detective, this Sherlock Holmes I told you about. That imposter made quite a good living from begging. When Officer Suzuki investigates this false priest he may find that this man was doing quite well playing the part of a mendicant. After all, he was aggressive in soliciting donations when the other priests in Karuizawa are quite passive."

I told this to Officer Suzuki. He asked, "But how could he know he was involved in the Abbot's death?"

"The other mendicant priests must have noticed this man," Sigerson-san answered. "Even if their religious convictions didn't allow them to aggressively confront him, they must have said something about him to the Abbot. I believe the Abbot was about to do something to unmask this false priest. I suspect that somehow this man got wind of this and went to the temple to confront the Abbot. I believe that the Abbot stood firm in his resolve to rid Karuizawa of this imposter. Because of that, this man used his walking staff to strike and kill the Abbot. Officer Suzuki saw an example of how quick-tempered this man is just a few moments ago when the man struck at him. By the way, if Officer Suzuki examines the man's walking stick with a magnifying glass he may find traces of blood on the stick. That would be the blood of the Abbot."

I translated this to Officer Suzuki and he immediately gathered up the man's walking stick for later examination.

"How did your conversation with the woman who lived near the temple confirm your deductions?" I asked Sigerson-san.

"That was elementary. Because the gravel in the temple courtyard was so disturbed, I could not see evidence of the original confrontation between this man and the Abbot. I could see, however, from the foot impressions in the courtyard gravel that the mendicant priests return to the Temple as a group. Since they returned as a group it was a simple deduction to understand they probably left as a group. When we talked to the woman sweeping in front of her house she mentioned she had seen a priest as part of the parade of passers-by. She was so used to seeing priests that she did not note that it was unusual for a lone priest to walk past her house. This man was that lone priest. He was leaving the temple after killing the Abbot."

When I finished translating for Officer Suzuki, he stood stiffly and gave Sigerson-san a deep and formal bow.

"That is Officer Suzuki's way of thanking you," I explained to Sigerson-san. "This has been an amazing demonstration of the power of your methods for both the Officer and me."

A brief smile flitted across Sigerson-san's face. He was pleased with the result of his investigation, as well he should be.

Later that evening Hosokawa-san prepared a celebratory feast. In a small place like Karuizawa it was soon known that both Sigerson-san and I were involved in the capture of the Abbot's murderer and Hosokawa-san apparently felt some show of congratulation was appropriate. Hosokawa-san prepared *sashimi*, which Sigerson-san eyed balefully, but he ate the raw fish without comment, as well as *sekihan* and *tai*, the traditional red beans and rice and fish that are served at a celebratory meal.

I was very pleased with Hosokawa-san's generous preparation of a special meal to honor Sigerson-san's accomplishment until she brought out a large bowl from the kitchen and placed it ceremoniously in front of Sigerson-san. It was a bowl of butter. Before I could admonish Hosokawa-san, however, Sigerson-san's actions prevented me from doing so. Believe it or not, that henna gaijin took a large pat of the butter and placed it to melt over his bowl of red beans and rice!

The Case of the Devil's Voice

Words sound in my head.

Voices tell me the future.

Truth or the Devil?

"I think my husband is going mad."

When a physician is told this he must consider two possibilities. One is that the woman's husband may indeed be going mad. The other possibility is that the woman herself may be mad. Looking at Itoh-sama, I was not sure which was true.

Itoh-sama sat in my surgery wearing an expensive gray silk kimono. Painted on the hem of the kimono was a meandering blue and white stream flanked by green shoots and purple irises, in keeping with the season. A pale yellow *obi* picked up some of the color from the interior of the iris, a subtle reminder of the sunshine that follows the spring rains that nourish the iris. For most people a kimono of this quality would be a family treasure but for Itoh-sama it was simply everyday wear.

The elegant effect of her kimono, however, was spoiled by the rest of her appearance. Her face was haggard with dark circles under her eyes. Her hair was carefully coiffed, but the perfection you would expect from a woman of her class was marred by stray strands sticking out at odd angles. This was explained because she would nervously touch at her hair with hands that had a slight tremble to them, causing strands to come adrift. Her voice vacillated from a tone that implied familiarity with giving a house full of servants orders to a dry, cracked whisper that seemed tinged with fear. This, indeed, was a woman either driven to desperation because of all the fears she had for her husband or a woman who was starting to slip into madness herself. Perhaps she was both.

It occurred to me that Sigerson-san could probably tell the difference using his remarkable powers of observation and deduction, but I could hardly bring him into my surgery to observe Itoh-sama. Besides, Itoh-sama was naturally speaking Japanese and Sigerson-san would not be able to understand her.

I sat back in my chair and asked the obvious question. "Why do you think he is going mad, Itoh-sama?"

"I believe that he thinks he hears voices, Sensei."

"Voices?"

"Yes, in his head. I believe he is hearing voices. I think the voices tell him awful things. I think the voices are driving him mad."

I had heard of such cases when I studied medicine in England, primarily among the poor unfortunates who were in Bethlem Hospital in London, but I had never treated one. Here in Japan we tend not to talk about this madness, thinking it will taint the reputation of the entire family, so it was an extraordinary admission for Itoh-sama to tell me her fears. It was a clear sign of the desperation she was feeling.

"What makes you think he hears voices, Itoh-sama?"

"I'm not totally sure he does. At the start of his strange behavior he would make vague allusions to voices telling him things and advising him on business matters, but he would never fully explain where and how he heard these voices. I was able to surmise that he thought the voices were supernatural and that if he spoke about them openly they would stop talking to him. At least I think that's what he believes. Regardless, his behavior has become increasingly bizarre and frightening."

"And when did his peculiar behavior start?"

"Soon after we came here to the Karuizawa area."

"And when was that, Itoh-sama?"

Itoh-sama sighed and fidgeted in her chair. That was a bad sign because normally I would expect her to sit calmly upright. Serenity, or at least the public appearance of serenity, was something instilled in women of her class from early childhood.

"Perhaps I should start at the beginning, Sensei," she said.

"That would helpful, Itoh-sama."

"Are you familiar with my husband's family, Sensei?"

"Oh course, Itoh-sama." Itoh is a common name, but the family that Itoh-sama married into have been *daimyou* royalty for hundreds of years. They were one of the families that backed the restoration of the Emperor twenty-five years ago, overturning the Shogunate that had ruled Japan for 250 years. After the Imperial restoration the Itoh family, like most noble families that backed the Emperor, were given various trade concessions and monopolies to reward them for their support, making these families extremely wealthy.

I used the honorific "sama" instead of the usual "san" with Itoh-sama, which was only polite and proper given her position. However, I was not intimidated by her. My own family was a samurai family, part of the Matsudaira clan. As you may know, the Matsudairas were a branch family of the Tokugawa Shogun's family.

Therefore, less than three decades ago, Itoh-sama's family helped destroy the system that my family supported.

"The Itoh family has three sons," Itoh-sama continued. "Shigenobu was the oldest, followed by my husband, Takayoshi, and his younger brother, Aritomo. As the first son Shigenobu was, of course, groomed to head the Itoh clan and to manage its many business interests. His younger brothers were allowed to pursue their interests. My husband had an interest in Japanese folklore and Aritomo was interested in Western shipbuilding. In due course Shigenobu became the head of the Itoh clan and shouldered all the business and family burdens that entailed.

"Tragically, a few years ago Shigenobu died suddenly in an accident. The responsibilities of the Itoh family were unexpectedly thrust on my husband, Takayoshi. Sensei, it was a terrible burden. The strain of being the head of the Itoh clan has changed my husband. Before he used to be quite even-tempered and happy. After assuming the responsibilities of the Itoh clan he became tense and stressed."

It was plain that Itoh-sama was used to being the center of any social group and that she liked to talk. I let her talk, observing her closely as she recounted her story.

"My husband's youngest brother Aritomo has maintained a summer villa in Karuizawa for several years. He uses it to escape the stifling heat and humidity of the Tokyo summers. A few months ago he informed us that the villa next to his was for sale. He suggested that we buy it, noting that with the new rail line to Tokyo running daily it would be easy to transport any important papers or communicate matters requiring my husband's attention.

"Because I thought the mountain air and scenery would help relax him, I encouraged my husband to act on his brother's idea. As a result we bought the villa and moved to Karuizawa two months ago.

"Since coming to Karuizawa my husband has not become more relaxed. On the contrary, he has become more tense and..." here she sought she proper word "...frightening."

"Frightening?"

She sighed. "Yes, Sensei, frightening. He hardly sleeps and he spends most of the daylight hours brooding or screaming at the servants for the slightest act that displeases him. He looks at me with the eyes of a devil and accuses me of terrible things, things I can't repeat."

"What does he do at night when he doesn't sleep?"

"He walks through the villa or roams the garden."

"Have you tried asking him what's wrong?" I knew it would be unusual for a wife to question her husband, no matter what the circumstances. Almost all marriages are arranged and sometimes the couples are neither close nor compatible. But still, under these conditions...

"Yes, just a week ago I worked up the courage to do so. He said I was prying into his business and ordered me to stop. Of course, I have obeyed my husband, but I have also become increasingly concerned about his health and the state of his mind. That is why I have come to you, Sensei. My husband has refused to see any of our doctors in Tokyo so I thought that a local doctor may be in a better position to observe my husband and offer advice. I was told that a specialist in Dutch Medicine may be especially good for troubles with the mind so I have come to you. I would like you to visit us at our villa for a few days and observe my husband to see if there is anything you can do to help him."

It was apparent that Itoh-sama expected a rapid acceptance of her proposal. With the position and wealth of the Itohs, most doctors would welcome a chance to act as a physician to them. I, however, had many reservations.

These reservations did not include the history of conflict between the Matsudaira clan and the Itoh clan, I might add. Japan is now united under the Emperor and the fights of the previous generation, no matter how recent and raw, do not affect my oath as a physician to help the sick.

Instead my reservations involved the particular circumstances presented by Itoh-sama's story. Based on my observations I had a strong feeling that Itoh-sama was telling the truth and was not the one who was mad. However, I also felt she was not telling the complete truth. In addition, it was not Lord Itoh who was asking for help, but his wife. It is always difficult to offer help to people who do not ask for it. Finally, in truth, the ability of Dutch Medicine to deal with troubles of the mind is highly over-rated. I did observe several mentally disturbed patients in London when I studied there but, except for patience and keeping the dangerous patients isolated from society, there were no cures that were proffered.

"There may be some difficulties..." I told Itoh-sama. This kind of hesitation was, of course, tantamount to a refusal among polite Japanese. I would not be so rude as to bluntly say no.

Itoh-sama flinched. For a woman trained from birth to maintain her composure it was as if I had struck her. At that moment I realized how desperate this woman was. I fleetingly wondered if Sigerson-san would have realized this through his observational powers. I quickly reconsidered my decision.

"Actually, Itoh-sama," I said, "the only difficulty is that I have a gaijin patient staying with me who is recovering from an illness. If your invitation to stay a few nights at your villa can be extended to this patient, Sigerson-san, then I can come and observe your husband and offer any advice I can."

Itoh-sama's face showed relief. "If it's necessary for you to bring a patient with you, Sensei, then this... Sig...Sig..."

"Sigerson-san."

"Ah, Sigerson-san. What strange names these gaijin have. In any case, he can certainly accompany you. We will say that you are coming to the villa to attend to me. My husband may get angry if he thinks you are there for him without his consent." Itoh-sama immediately brightened up at my compliance with her request and she regained her composure. She was used to being obeyed and my initial refusal to comply with her request had unsettled her more than it would another who was not so privileged.

The next day Sigerson-san and I were riding in the carriage that Itoh-sama had sent to transport us to their villa. I had conveyed the information Itoh-sama had given me to Sigerson-san and he seemed interested in what I told him, but made no comment. I did notice he seemed anxious to get to the Itoh villa, however, so I did not feel guilty about bringing him with me.

The trip from Karuizawa was uneventful. The mountain air was crisp and refreshing and we could smell the perfume of the pine trees that lined the road. Sigerson was silent and pensive on the journey, perhaps saving himself for what the end of the journey might present to us.

The carriage climbed a wooded hill and the driver informed me that we would soon be arriving. Through the trees we could see glimpses of a magnificent view into the valley below. We passed the fence and gate of a large villa and the driver said that it was the home of Aritomo-sama, the youngest Itoh brother. Right next door, at the very top of the hill, we came upon another Japanese-style gate. Waiting there were several servants and Itoh-sama. I must admit I was flattered to be greeted like an honored guest instead of simply a hired physician. It was obvious that

Itoh-sama was very skilled at enlisting the aid of people, even those who were not impressed by her money and position.

When I introduced Itoh-sama to Sigerson-san she looked up at him and said in English, "Hello. It is nice to meet you." She looked at me and asked me to explain to Sigerson-san that her English was minimal and confined to simple words.

Sigerson-san was at least three heads taller than Itoh-sama and it made an almost comical picture to see the tall gaijin standing by the short noblewoman. Of course, Sigerson-san was taller than any Japanese, including myself, but I judged he would be considered tall even in England, especially since his gaunt frame accentuated his height.

One of the maids showed us to our room. Since my own house had Japanese-style bedrooms, Sigerson-san was not surprised that our room had almost no furnishings. Our bedding, of course, would be laid out at bedtime.

The villa was in true Japanese style, with a magnificent black tile roof and expensive tatami and shouji throughout. The shape of the villa was rather like the letter "U", with a large garden contained between the two arms of the U. Our room was in one leg of the U. If the design of the villa was like others I had been in, the quarters for Lord Itoh and Itoh-sama would be in the other leg for privacy from visitors.

The shouji in our room opened onto the large garden. It was a Japanese garden, imitating nature without the groomed formality of a Chinese style garden. Our Japanese gardens are always well thought-out and tended like a Chinese garden, but we like a touch of wildness to remind us of the natural roots to all beauty.

One corner of the garden had a pool with a small island in it. The island had pines growing on it. The pines were the conventional symbols for cranes, indicating a long life. I could see a flash of white and red in the water telling me that *koi* were lurking under the surface.

"I see that there is a room for the Japanese tea ceremony in this villa," I remarked.

Sigerson-san's interest was immediately aroused. "How do you know that? Only our room has its screen open to the garden. How do you know that one of the other rooms in this building is devoted to the tea ceremony?"

My observation was one that any educated Japanese could make and I didn't think it was especially remarkable. Yet to Sigerson-san, who lacked knowledge of Japanese culture, it must have been as mysterious as the deductions Sigerson-san could make about people, places and events with no obvious clues, except to him. I enjoyed the opportunity to act as the teacher. It must be the same pleasure Sigerson-san feels when he explains his deductions to others.

"Do you see that rock with the basin for water carved into it?" I pointed to the far side of the garden.

"Yes."

"That is a *chozubachi*. It is used for washing your hands before entering a teahouse. This garden doesn't have a separate teahouse, so a room near the chozubachi must be used for the tea ceremony. Are you familiar with the tea ceremony, Sigerson-san?"

"No, I am not. I have heard of it but I don't know what it entails."

"Perhaps we can participate in one together some day. You may find it interesting."

A maid came and asked us to join Lord Itoh and Itoh-sama for tea. "We're going to go to another kind of tea ceremony," I said.

Sigerson-san gave me a quizzical look and I continued, "I am making a kind of joke. The maid has just asked us to join Lord Itoh and Itoh-sama for tea, which means a formal introduction to his Lordship."

"Does custom require me to do anything?"

"No, I will translate whatever discussion occurs. I will try to evaluate Lord Itoh from a medical perspective but I would appreciate any insights you might have about his behavior when we are together in private again."

"Certainly."

The maid guided us to a formal reception room near the entrance to the villa. Before we reached it Itoh-sama appeared. The maid immediately dropped to her knees and bowed her head in an old-fashioned greeting to her mistress. I was a little surprised at the formality of the Itoh household but, as wealthy nobility, I imagine they chose to live with the stuffiness of a former age. I couldn't imagine Hosokawa-san, my own housekeeper, showing such formal obeisance every time I appeared in my house.

"I wanted to warn you," Itoh-sama said. "My husband is having a bad time of it. Things are so serious I asked his brother Aritomo to join us, hoping that he will have more influence on my husband than I have."

Itoh-sama turned to go before I could get more information about her husband's condition. Sigerson-san and I followed the maid as she showed us the entrance to the reception room. She got to her knees, slid the shouji open, and bowed so Sigerson-san and I could enter.

The Itoh villa reception room was a bit rustic, in keeping with a mountain villa. It was a 14-mat room so it was spacious, but it was not decorated with the gorgeous paintings on the screens and ceilings that you might expect from a family with the Itohs' wealth. Instead it had a simple *tokonoma* alcove containing a single vase with a red *tsubaki*, camellia blossom.

Sitting in the room was a man in his late thirties, dressed in an expensive brown kimono. Naturally I gave him a polite bow as we entered and he formally bowed back. I saw three zabuton cushions were lined up along one side with two others in front of the tokonoma. The man was sitting on one of the three cushions so these were intended for the Itohs. Sigerson-san and I were given the place of honor in front of the alcove. The maid slid the shouji back into place, blocking our view of the corridor.

I sat on the zabuton in proper fashion, with my legs tucked under me. Sigerson-san asked, "What should I do? I am not cognizant of the customs for this type of meeting."

"Simply sit. You don't have to try and sit as I am, but please don't extend your legs with the soles of your feet towards that gentleman or the alcove. That would be impolite."

Sigerson sat down crossing his long legs in what we call Burmese fashion. A maid entered the room with a cherry-wood tray. On it she had teacups with covers, sitting on a saucer. The teacups were an intense indigo in color and had a pine pattern on them. Sigerson-san lifted the cover of his cup and looked at the green ocha inside. I knew from experience at my house that he preferred black tea, koucha, instead. He put the lid back on the cup with a distinct disdain.

I bowed once again to the gentleman and said, "My name is Doctor Junichi Watanabe. This is my patient, Sigerson-san."

"I am Itoh Aritomo. Itoh-sama told me she enlisted your help to examine my brother, Lord Itoh. Itoh-sama said

I was supposed to pretend that you are here to attend to her, which I am happy to do. I don't want to upset my elder brother because he has insisted on not seeking medical help for his current state of mind. I hope you can help him, Sensei, because the future of our clan rests on his abilities."

As Aritomo-san finished speaking there was a commotion in the corridor. It was the loud voice of a man arguing with a woman who was, from her voice, Itoh-sama. Their voices would rise and fall, with most of their words indistinct. Some words could be understood, though, such as "guests," "why," and "gaijin." They were obviously arguing about Sigerson-san and me. Aritomo-san and I kept our eyes forward and unfocussed, with a neutral expression on our faces, drawing the mental screens across our visages that allow Japanese to pretend we haven't heard what is clearly there to hear.

Sigerson-san was not as polite. He watched the shouji with his hawk-like eyes, peering intently and apparently trying to make sense of what the raised voices in the corridor meant. Finally, the voices quieted and, after a slight pause, the shouji was slid back by the maid and Lord Itoh and Itoh-sama entered.

Itoh-sama was flustered but had enough composure to bow to us politely. Lord Itoh stomped into the reception chamber glaring at us, rudely going to sit on his zabuton without giving us so much as a nod.

My face flushed with anger at such treatment but I remembered our purpose and kept my composure. Sigerson-san was blissfully unaware we had just been insulted. Instead he was studying Lord Itoh.

Lord Itoh was wearing an expensive gray kimono with the Itoh clan crest on the sleeves and shoulders. He had a folded fan tucked in his sash and his feet were clad in white *tabi*, socks. His face was long with a thin nose and he wore an expression as though he was smelling something kusai, stinky.

During my brief visit to Bethlem Hospital as part of my studies in London, I was told by the warden that true madness could be seen in the eyes. I wasn't completely convinced this was true, but it was certainly true in Lord Itoh's case. His eyes blazed with some inner torment. The fire in his eyes contrasted sharply with the rest of his face, which was puffy and saggy, with deep black bags under his eyes.

"I understand you are here to treat my wife," Lord Itoh said to me. He said it sharply, as you would talk to a low servant. Itoh-sama looked at me with a combination of embarrassment and pleading, clearly asking me to overlook Lord Itoh's rudeness.

I smiled, bowed slightly, and said, "I am Doctor Watanabe Junichi. Yes, Itoh-sama asked me to attend to her." I intentionally didn't add his name and title when addressing him. It was a small slight, but a pointed one that didn't escape his attention. His eyes narrowed and I told myself to contain my own emotions for the sake of studying this disturbed man.

"And who is this gaijin?" Lord Itoh pointed to Sigerson-san with a motion of his chin.

"He is a patient that I am caring for, Lord Itoh. His name is Sigerson-san. He is a Norwegian visiting Japan. I brought him because I must still attend to him as he recovers from an illness. He is under my care because I am a doctor of Dutch Medicine."

Lord Itoh's eyes narrowed and he seemed to get very excited. "Does Dutch Medicine teach you about ghosts?"

"Ghosts, Lord Itoh?"

"What did he ask?" Sigerson-san asked, sensitive to the tone of my response.

"He asked me about ghosts." If Sigerson-san had a reaction to this bizarre question he was able to mask it.

"No, Lord Itoh, we receive no special training regarding ghosts."

Lord Itoh looked disappointed. "Ghosts can be a difficult subject. I am an expert on folklore and I know that ghosts can be very tricky. Sometimes they mean well for the humans they contact, giving them good advice and counsel. Other times they can be evil, like the malevolent spirit in *The Tale of Genji*. How can one know if it is a helpful spirit or a Devil speaking to you? Does Dutch Medicine give you any advice on how you can know that?"

"No, Lord Itoh, it does not," I had to admit.

He immediately seemed to lose interest in the interview and said, "Very well. Stay and attend to my wife, if you must. I have family business to attend to." He stood and left the room.

As soon as we could hear Lord Itoh's footsteps fading down the corridor, Aritomo-san turned to me and sighed. "I must apologize for my older brother's rudeness, Sensei. As you can tell, he is a troubled man. I have been encouraging my sister-in-law to summon our family doctors from Tokyo to examine my brother. I am happy that she has started by obtaining the services of a local doctor. That is a good first step." The way Aritomo-san said this made it clear that he had little faith in a 'local doctor' and that the first step would not be the last step.

"What do you think, Sensei?" Itoh-sama asked.

As part of my training in Dutch Medicine I had been taught that patients don't like indecision or confusion. I was uncertain about Lord Itoh's condition, given the brief exposure I had to him. Instead of giving a hazy opinion I fell back on one of the tricks I had been taught. Instead of answering I asked more questions.

"Was this his normal behavior before coming here?"

"Sensei, my husband was the most gentle and polite of men. He was a Japanese folklore scholar before the death of his brother Shigenobu thrust him into the leadership of the Itoh clan. He would never be as rude as he was just now if he was himself. I know you found his remarks about ghosts strange. He was always interested in folklore but lately he has become obsessed with ghosts, reading everything he can obtain on the subject and talking about them constantly."

"And this change occurred just since he arrived here?"

"This focus on ghosts happened just since we arrived at this villa."

"Was there any incident or event that might cause this? Perhaps a fall or some accidental blow to the head?"

"No, none."

"He was always a little different, even as a young man," Aritomo-san interjected. "Perhaps the right word is that he was strange, because he never took interest in the family business. He was always immersed in books, reading about ghosts and devils and other folklore. This was totally useless information. I study, too, but I study Western shipbuilding because it is useful for our family trading business. When our elder brother Shigenobu died and the full weight of the Itoh family fell on my middle brother's shoulders... well, perhaps it was all too much for him. I haven't talked to my sister-in-law about this, but brother has also been making strange decisions about the family business. It has us all worried about brother's ability to cope with the pressures he's under."

"I can see he is under tremendous stress. Do you think it's the family business that is putting him under stress or is there something else?"

"The burdens of the family have been heavy on him," Itoh-sama said, "but there is something else, something that torments him and prevents him from sleeping."

I was obviously puzzled and disturbed by this. I could see that Itoh-sama and Aritomo-san were both looking at me expectantly, waiting for some sage pronouncement from the doctor. I fell back on my medical training. I decided to show patience and observe closely because this was a case I couldn't immediately understand.

I put on my wisest face and said, "Thank you for that information. From a short interview like this I can't give a definitive diagnosis. I would like to wait a few days and observe Lord Itoh some more. It would be extremely helpful, Itoh-sama, if you could also convince Lord Itoh to allow me to give him a physical examination. Perhaps you can say I have helped you with Dutch Medicine and perhaps I should look at him, too, since I am here."

That seemed to satisfy Itoh-sama, but Aritomo-san said, "But you must have some preliminary observations. Tokyo doctors certainly would have a diagnosis by now. What are your conclusions?"

I sighed. "A sudden change in demeanor is always a sign of some change in the mental or physical status of a patient. If we can rule out some physical cause, then we must face the possibility that perhaps the strain of the family business may be too much for Lord Itoh."

That seemed to satisfy Aritomo-san and frighten Itoh-sama. I made the usual polite conventions and excused

Sigerson-san and me. I had much to think about and wanted to see if Sigerson-san had any observations to make.

Sigerson-san remained silent until we returned to our room. Then he wanted a detailed description of what had been said. I gave him a synopsis of what was said, but he responded, "Forgive me, Doctor, but can you remember, as near as possible, exactly what each person said? It would be helpful if I knew the exact words." Therefore, I tried to give him a word-for-word recounting of our conversation.

"Do you think Lord Itoh is mad?" Sigerson-san asked me when I was finished.

"He is certainly rude and strange but I am not sure if he is mad. There can be many causes for a sudden change in behavior, such as the one Lord Itoh has experienced. Some may be because of a physical injury and some may have to do with some stress or damage to his mind."

"And what do you think of his talk about ghosts and devils?"

"You must understand, Sigerson-san, that virtually everyone in Japan believes in ghosts and most believe in devils. Our two religions, Shinto and Buddhism, believe that the souls of the dead continue to have a presence. We even have a Buddhist festival called *obon* at the end of summer when the souls of the departed come close to those of us still here on earth. I know in Europe most Christians believe that souls go to heaven or hell, but many Europeans also believe in ghosts. During my time in England I was told many stories about ghosts that haunt castles and old manor houses. I was even told that the ghost of Queen Boleyn haunts the Tower of London."

Sigerson-san gave a small smile at this reference, although I don't know why. He said, "But surely as a man of science you don't believe in the supernatural."

"As a man of science I believe in keeping an open mind. More importantly, I find it comforting to think I can speak to my ancestors or my dead wife."

Our discussion was interrupted by a maid delivering our dinner trays. As I expected, it was an elegant *kaiseki* feast with delicate seasonal dishes. The vegetables were cunningly shaped and carved to look like flowers, leaves and small insects, each residing in a costly and exquisitely colored dish. Sigerson-san looked at the tray closely and sampled a few dishes. Gaijin often say Japanese kaiseki food looks better than it tastes and Sigerson-san's expression made me think he might share this opinion.

Sigerson-san looked at the cup of ocha on his tray and asked me, "Is there any proper English tea available?" By this I think Sigerson-san meant more than koucha. The English sometimes drink their tea with a slice of lemon or, although this may be hard to believe, even with milk and sugar in it! In fact, the lower classes in England drink a tea brewed so coarse and strong that the liquid that results is hardly recognizable as koucha.

I asked the maid if black tea was available. She bowed until her head touched the tatami mat. "I'm sorry, Sensei-sama, but Lord Itoh prefers only ocha and doesn't keep koucha at this villa. At his main home in Tokyo, of course, we have many teas to serve but at this vacation house we have only a limited supply of things for guests. I deeply apologize for not having koucha. I hope you will try the ocha, however. It is from the Ippodo tea shop in Kyoto."

Ippodo is one of the oldest and best suppliers of ocha, so if Sigerson-san did not like this ocha, then he probably did not care for green tea of any type. I dismissed the maid, who was still making apologies over the tea, and explained the situation to Sigerson-san. He looked disappointed but said no more.

After a dinner that he only picked at, Sigerson-san took out a pipe and filled it with tobacco. He went to sit in a corner of the room, puffing slowly. "Aren't you going to eat more?" I asked him. "I know some of the things in the dinner are strange to you, but you might find some things to your liking."

"I'm sorry, Doctor, but I often skip meals entirely when I am immersed in a difficult problem. Please continue eating and don't mind me. I might have to smoke several pipes before I understand what is happening."

True to his word, Sigerson-san continued puffing on his pipe, showing no apparent signs of hunger. Shrugging, I started eating the sumptuous meal, eating Sigerson-san's share of a few of the more delicious dishes.

After dinner the maid returned and made up our beds. She lit a candle between them and withdrew. Sigerson-san stopped smoking his pipe and, after making our evening preparations, Sigerson-san and I went to bed. It had been a full and somewhat tiring day.

Later that night I awoke.

I realized that, strangely enough, it was darkness that woke me. The candle was extinguished and I could hear Sigerson-san moving about in the dark. I surmised that he had put out the candle. The reason for this soon became clear as Sigerson-san slid the shouji that faced the garden open slightly. He obviously didn't want someone to see the light spilling from the open shouji.

I got out of bed and moved to the partially open shouji. In the starlight coming through the opening I could see Sigerson-san crouched at the shouji, peering through the narrow gap he had created. When he sensed me approaching he put his finger to his lips to indicate I should be quiet. I also looked through the narrow gap of the partially open shouji.

I heard him before my eyes adjusted enough for me to see him. "Shigenobu! Shigenobu!" It was an anguished wail, like a wounded animal. It sent a chill up my spine, unnerving me. I gave a quick glance at Sigerson-san and, as near as I could perceive in the dim light, he seemed completely calm and unmoved.

"Shigenobu!" The sound came again. It was the name of Lord Itoh's older brother. In the garden I saw movement. It was a dark figure, wandering erratically through the garden, dashing from bush to bush and tree to tree, stopping to freeze momentarily and then darting in a new direction. It reminded me of some giant, dark bird.

Presently the figure came close enough to our vantage point for us to make out its visage. It was Lord Itoh, his face twisted in anguish and fear, with a wild look in his eyes discernable even in the pale starlight. I shrunk back instinctively from the crack in the shouji but Sigerson-san stood his ground. I immediately realized that Sigerson-san's reaction was the correct one because movement would be more noticeable in these conditions than staying still. I froze.

Lord Itoh glanced our way for a fraction of a second, and then he darted away, moving deeper into the garden. We waited for several minutes to see if he would return but the garden returned to darkened stillness.

Eventually, Sigerson-san shut the shouji and said, "I believe that will be it for tonight. We can return to sleep, Doctor. What was Lord Itoh saying?"

"He was saying Shigenobu, the name of his dead brother. I suppose this behavior was what his wife was referring to when she thought he was going mad. Perhaps he is mad."

In the darkened room, with the starlight shut out by the closed shouji, I couldn't see the expression on Sigerson-san's face. But there was no mistaking the deadly seriousness of his tone. "I believe that Lord Itoh is not mad. But he is in the grip of evil. A malignant, destructive evil has manifested itself in the guise of a devil. I believe we have a duty to eliminate the evil that has gripped him." His words sent a chill through my entire body. I had told Sigerson-san that I believed in ghosts and devils, but to have a man as rational as Sigerson-san confirm that we were in close proximity to such evil was frightening.

"From your comments earlier I assumed that you didn't believe in devils," I said.

"A devil can take many forms," Sigerson-san replied cryptically.

I tried to get him to elaborate but Sigerson-san didn't want to continue the discussion. Instead, he suggested that we go back to sleep because we had work to do the next morning. I still had many questions about what we saw and Sigerson-san's reaction to it but I had started to trust his instincts in this type of situation so I withheld my questions and eventually went back to sleep.

Early the next morning Sigerson-san was already dressed when I awoke. "I'm sorry to trouble you, Doctor, but if you can get dressed I would like you to give me a tour of the garden."

Based on the events of the previous night this seemed a strange request but I decided to comply with Sigerson-san's desires. As we started walking through the garden at the Itoh villa, however, Sigerson-san seemed to have little interest in my commentary on the garden's plants and design. Instead he seemed to have an inordinate interest in the paths of the garden. When I was in England I somehow got the impression that Norwegians were a people focused on the sea, but I had learned that Sigerson-san was a Norwegian who had all the legendary tracking skills of the native Indian population of North America, so I knew he was trying to read what the footprints on the paths told him. I stopped my commentary and simply followed Sigerson-san through the garden.

As we approached the chozubachi Sigerson-san said, "You told me this has something to do with the tea ceremony?"

"Yes. It's a stone basin for washing your hands."

He studied the ground in front of the basin. "Is it common to pray in front of it?"

"Pray? No. It is an implement for the tea ceremony."

"Do you know why Lord Itoh might kneel in front of it?"

"Kneel? Is this why you asked me about prayer?"

"Yes." He pointed to two depressions in the sandy path that, I suppose, could have been caused by the knees of someone kneeling.

I thought for a moment, then said, "The tea ceremony is a very important ritual, but I don't know why someone would be praying in front of a chozubachi basin. Remember, Sigerson-san, in Japan we kneel for something as simple as drinking a cup of tea, so prayer does not have to be involved. In fact, most of our praying is done either standing or sitting, not kneeling as they do in the West."

He thought about this for a moment, then said, "And what are those for?" Sigerson-san pointed to a bamboo ladle and a large section of bamboo that were resting near the basin.

"The ladle is used to pour water for washing your hands but I'm not sure what the section of bamboo is for." I picked up the piece of bamboo and looked at it. It was hollow like a pipe and this clue allowed me to discern its use.

"I believe there's a *suikinkutsu* in this garden," I said, surprised.

Sigerson-san already had a quizzical look on his face before I could start my explanation.

"It's a rare thing these days and actually most Japanese wouldn't know what it is anymore. I saw one once in a garden in Shinagawa, near Tokyo, and it was explained to me. The word means 'water *koto* cave.' A koto is a Japanese musical instrument, rather like the western zither. Here, let me confirm a suikinkutsu exists."

I took the bamboo pipe and placed it with one end on the pebbles that were just in front of the water basin. Then I took a ladle of water and poured it on the pebbles. Then I crouched down and put my ear to the other end of the pipe.

Ping! Ping! Ping!

Through the pipe came a distinctive, echoing sound, like the taut string of a koto being plucked in the midst of a large cave. I motioned to Sigerson-san to place his ear to the bamboo pipe so he could hear for himself. He bent his tall body down so his ear was next to the bamboo and I poured another ladle of water on the pebbles.

"Remarkable," he said. "What causes that sound?"

"Under the pebbles there is an earthenware pot buried upside down. A small hole is drilled in the pot so the water works its way through the pebbles and drips into the hollow cavity inside the pot. The garden designer partially fills the inside of the pot with clay and rocks so the dripping water makes the pinging sound. The designer can actually adjust the tone by how full the jar is. When heard through this bamboo pipe it sounds like water dripping in a large cave. That's the distinctive ringing sound we call *suikinon*. It's almost a lost art to construct one of these now, so I don't know if this suikinkutsu is a modern one or perhaps one constructed hundreds of years ago."

"Fascinating," Sigerson-san said. "Can you pour another ladle of water?"

I complied with another ladle of water and, for some reason, a smile crossed Sigerson-san's face. He seemed to immediately lose interest in examining the garden. He stood up and started walking to our room.

"Will the maid bring us breakfast if we ask her?" Sigerson-san inquired, looking back over his shoulder.

I was baffled by Sigerson-san's sudden change. I've noticed that gaijin often have a short attention span but Sigerson-san had remarkable powers of concentration. Sigerson-san was more mercurial than most people, but he obviously understood something that I did not when he heard the sound of the suikinkutsu.

I took another ladle of water and poured it on the pebbles. When I placed my ear to the bamboo pipe the sound of the dripping water was exactly the same. As far as I could tell there was no change in pitch, tone, or the echo that made it sound like notes played in a large cave. I tried another ladle of water with the same result. As far as I could detect, there was no change. Yet something about that second ladle of water had satisfied Sigerson-san and sent him off in another direction for his investigation. What could it be? I racked my brain but I couldn't understand why Sigerson lost interest in exploring the garden upon hearing it.

I eventually stopped trying to understand Sigerson-san's motivation and followed him back to our room. In less than half an hour we were eating breakfast. After his earnest pronouncements about devils the night before, he seemed to lose all interest and just wanted to eat, although he again looked balefully at the green tea served him.

After breakfast Sigerson-san told me he wanted to take a walk, so he went off on his own while I conferred with Itoh-sama. She confided that although she slept in a separate room from Lord Itoh she was aware of his nocturnal wanderings.

"It has gotten progressively worse, Sensei," she told me. "Last night was the worst episode yet. I heard him calling his brother's name. Perhaps the death of his brother has affected him more deeply than I imagined. I thought it was the pressure of running the family business that was weighing on him but now I realize he's mad with grief, too. My brother-in-law, Aritomo-san, is so concerned that he told me yesterday that he will send for doctors from Tokyo regardless of what you recommend, Sensei." She bowed. "I'm sorry. Please don't take this as an insult but I feel he might be right. I don't know if I can watch my husband descend into madness without doing something."

I said the usual words of understanding and comfort that doctors are taught to say but I never felt as helpless as that moment. Doctors can fix broken limbs but we have not yet learned to fix broken minds. I returned to my room dejected.

Late that afternoon Sigerson-san returned looking rather pleased with himself. It was frankly annoying to see him looking so smug when I hoped that he would help me with this situation with Lord Itoh, but naturally I kept my temper and tried to be pleasant, despite what I was feeling. Even if we failed with Lord Itoh, Sigerson-san was a guest in my house and would remain so for some unknown period to come. I, of course, wanted to maintain harmonious relations with him despite his baffling attitude.

My annoyance changed after our dinner, however, when he said to me, "If you give me some help, Doctor, I think we will be able to expose the devil stalking Lord Itoh."

"Are you serious?" I asked Sigerson-san.

"Extremely serious. As serious as the evil that has been perpetrated in this villa."

"How can I help?" I asked.

Later that night the garden was dark and still, the stars providing the only light. A shouji screen in the private wing of the manor slid open silently. Lord Itoh looked through the gap in the screen into the garden. He stood for a moment and looked around. All was silent and he saw no movement so he walked out of the house and advanced into the garden. Hesitating, almost reluctant, he walked towards the stone tea ceremony water basin in the garden. As he reached the chozubachi he took the ladle and poured the water onto the pebbles at the base of the basin. Then he knelt and took the bamboo pipe, placed one end on the pebbles, and put his ear to the pipe so he could hear.

After a few moments he gave a low groan and murmured, "Shigenobu…is it really you? Or are you some devil who is leading me to destruction and madness? How can I know? Who can tell me?"

I stood up from the bush were I had been crouching, watching the entire scene by the faint glow of starlight. "I think I can tell you, Lord Itoh," I said.

Lord Itoh gave a cry of surprise and dropped the bamboo pipe. He stood and started to run.

"Don't flee, Lord Itoh," I said hastily. "I know the voice that identified himself as your brother Shigenobu told you not to reveal his communications. I was told about it by someone else. You have not revealed the secret."

"Who… who could possibly tell you about the voice?"

"My friend, the gaijin Sigerson-san." As I said this I realized that, despite his many irritating habits, I actually did consider Sigerson-san a friend.

"How could a gaijin know that?"

"If things have gone according to plan he will be able to tell you himself."

I picked up the bamboo tube and placed it over the pebbles. I could hear the pinging of the water in the suikinkutsu, but I could also hear another voice, distant but distinct. "Doctor Watanabe, if you can hear me please join me."

I gave the tube to Lord Itoh and gestured for him to listen. Tentatively, he placed the tube on the pebbles and put his ear to it. A look of total shock crossed his face. "What is this?" he stammered. "It's speaking *Eigo*, English!"

"It's Sigerson-san asking me to join him. You should come, too, so you can meet the devil."

"So the voice wasn't my brother? It was a devil?"

"Actually, it was both."

I gave Lord Itoh no further explanation. Instead I led him from his garden and into the garden of the villa next door, the one owned by Aritomo-san. There I found Aritomo and Sigerson-san standing next to the fence that separated the two villas. Aritomo-san was boiling over in anger. It was dark so I could not see his complexion, but I was willing to wager it was fiery red with emotion.

"How dare you invade my private garden! Even for a gaijin this is unacceptable. This is outrageous!" Sigerson-san simply looked at Aritomo-san with the bland look of cold indifference. I suppose it helped that Sigerson-san didn't know what Aritomo-san was saying, but from the shouting and tone of his voice it must have been obvious what Aritomo-san was protesting. Sigerson-san simply didn't care. He would not be diverted from the truth.

"I'm sorry, Aritomo-san, but Sigerson-san doesn't speak Japanese so your expressions of outrage are being wasted. Besides, if I may say so, what is outrageous is driving your brother to the brink of madness."

"What are you talking about?" he blustered. "My brother may have the title in the family but I am still an Itoh and you should watch your language when addressing me."

"You well know what this is about, but for the sake of Lord Itoh I will have Sigerson-san explain. I will translate for him."

Aritomo-san looked apprehensive and Lord Itoh simply looked dazed. I asked Sigerson-san to explain.

"When Itoh-sama visited Doctor Watanabe and said she thought Lord Itoh was going mad, she imparted three important pieces of information. The first was that she thought Lord Itoh was hearing voices. The second was Lord Itoh's change in behavior started when he came to this vacation villa in Karuizawa. The third was that Lord Itoh's brother, Aritomo, was the one who found this villa. I did not believe these three things were unrelated."

I translated this into Japanese but omitted the part about Itoh-sama telling me that she thought her husband was going mad. There was no sense in upsetting Lord Itoh further by telling him his wife had betrayed a family confidence to a stranger, albeit the stranger was a doctor.

"Therefore, if the problems besetting Lord Itoh were not those caused by his own mind, there was a high probability that Aritomo Itoh was involved. At this stage I didn't know what was happening or how it was being accomplished.

"After our brief interview with Lord Itoh many things became clearer. Aritomo was anxious to have Lord Itoh declared mentally incompetent and he seemed irritated that Dr. Watanabe wouldn't immediately agree to this. I'm not familiar with Japanese family matters, but I assume that Aritomo would control the family businesses if Lord Itoh was judged incompetent, and he may even assume the family title, too.

"By the way," Sigerson-san said, looking at the Itohs, "you seem to place great store in Tokyo doctors but I would say that a doctor like Dr. Watanabe, who is prepared to be patient and gather information until he is sure of his diagnosis, is a superior physician. More importantly, I believe that Aritomo Itoh has talked to the doctors in Tokyo and they are predisposed to find Lord Itoh incompetent, even though he is quite sane."

Aritomo-san stammered a heated denial when I (with a little embarrassment over the praise for me) translated this. It was plain from the tone of Aritomo-san's voice, however, that Sigerson-san had hit home.

"Last night we observed Lord Itoh in the garden of his villa," Sigerson-san continued. "He was calling his elder brother's name and was in great distress. The question was why?

"We looked at the garden in the morning but the only fresh footprints I saw were from Lord Itoh. If no one else was in the garden, how could Lord Itoh hear things which distressed him? When I heard the musical instrument in the garden I knew the answer.

"Dr. Watanabe was kind enough to explain how the device in the garden, the water koto, works. He said that it was now unusual to have such a device and that many Japanese would not be familiar with it." Sigerson-san looked at Lord Itoh. "If I may say so, Lord Itoh, you are very lucky that Dr. Watanabe understood how that device worked.

"The Doctor told me the instrument is a vessel or pot buried underground with a carefully designed cavity in it. Water drips through a hole in the pot and forms the distinctive sound that is magnified by the bamboo pipe. I had Dr. Watanabe pour two ladles of water into the instrument and I noted that the sound did not change. This meant that water was not building up in the instrument. If water was filling the pot, then the tone would change, just as the sound of water being poured into a glass changes. I concluded there must be a drainpipe leading from the instrument and I spent much of today searching for the outlet to that drainpipe. I found it here, right at the fence that separates the two villas." Sigerson-san pointed to a round earthenware pipe poking under the fence, barely visible in the pale starlight.

"You, Aritomo, knew about this pipe. It led you to form a diabolical plan to deprive your brother of his position as the head of the House of Itoh. You knew your voice would carry through the pipe back to the musical instrument, then it would travel up the pipe of bamboo to your brother's ear. This is very much like the speaking tubes found in Western ships, and I understand you have an interest in Western shipbuilding. When he listened to that musical instrument, Lord Itoh also heard a voice claiming to be his dead brother."

"Aritomo told me the sound of the suikinkutsu would be most charming at night," Lord Itoh said. "That's why I started listening to it when I took my evening walk. It's true that I heard a voice that claimed to be my dead brother. The voice warned me not to tell others the details of what I heard and it told me that I should resign my position as head of the Itoh family and make Aritomo the head. I thought it was the voice of my elder brother berating me for being an unworthy successor. The voice constantly criticized me for every business decision I made and attacked me as being weak and incapable of running the family. It was driving me mad to hear my elder brother telling me to give up the position I inherited. I didn't know what to do. I didn't know if it was Shigenobu or some evil spirit; the ghost of my brother or a devil. It made me rude and short tempered because I was torn with indecision about what action I should take."

When I translated this for Sigerson-san, he said, "It's just as I thought. Aritomo only had to wait by this pipe until he saw water trickling out of it, then he could communicate with Lord Itoh, pretending to be a ghost. That was how I found him tonight, bent down by the pipe talking into it.

"I'm sure Aritomo thought Lord Itoh's interest in folklore would make him more susceptible to the advice of his elder brother coming from the grave. I'm not familiar with Japanese folklore but in Europe we have many stories of evil spirits pretending to be helpful before they reveal themselves as malevolent. I'm sure Japanese folklore must have the same. Ironically these stories made Lord Itoh more prone to question who was really talking to him, instead of simply accepting it. He knew that the voice might actually be a devil, not his brother." Sigerson-san looked directly at Aritomo-san and continued. "Now we have confirmed who it was talking to Lord Itoh. It actually was a devil; his brother."

We left Lord Itoh to solve this uncomfortable family situation with his brother and returned to our rooms. The next morning we were invited to have breakfast with Lord Itoh and Itoh-sama. We were presented with a very different couple than the one we saw at our first interview. Lord Itoh seemed rested and was punctiliously polite. Itoh-sama seemed relaxed and fully composed for the first time since I met her.

The Itohs thanked Sigerson-san and me numerous times and we, of course, told them our help was a small thing and not to worry about it.

"I feel a great weight has been lifted off me," Lord Itoh declared. "At last, for the first time since I came here, my mind is clear enough for me to conduct a tea ceremony. If you and Sigerson-san would like to stay, you are welcome to join us this afternoon for the ceremony."

I translated this for Sigerson-san and he said, "Can you convey my deepest apologies to Lord Itoh for me? I have a pressing need to return to the town of Karuizawa and this need will prevent me from attending the Japanese tea ceremony."

When I told Lord Itoh this, he said he would put the carriage at our disposal for our return to Karuizawa. He also said that I would be his official physician during his stays at his mountain villa. This was quite a shock to me. Such an appointment would greatly increase my stature in the Karuizawa community and would immensely help my practice. I stammered my thanks.

I reflected on the fact that my family and the Itoh family were on opposite sides of the recent revolution to depose the Shogun and restore the Emperor, but now Lord Itoh was bestowing a great honor on me, even though it was Sigerson-san who solved the mystery of the devil's voice. Perhaps old wounds can be healed to create a united Japan.

As we went back to our room at the Itoh villa to gather our things for the trip home I asked Sigerson-san, "What is the urgent business in Karuizawa that caused you to turn down the invitation to Lord Itoh's tea ceremony? A real tea ceremony is uniquely Japanese and you might have found it interesting."

"Someday I would like to experience a Japanese tea ceremony," Sigerson-san said, "but now I would like to go to the Mampei Hotel where I will treat you to scones, clotted cream, jam, finger sandwiches, biscuits, and plenty of strong, black tea. That is an English tea ceremony, and after a few days of green tea I am sorely in need of one!"

A month later I read that Aritomo Itoh was dispatched to the Itoh family's Indonesian office to oversee the operations there. The newspaper article said that although the Itohs' Indonesian operations were small, Lord Itoh must be planning a major expansion or he would not have dispatched his brother. The paper speculated that perhaps Aritomo-san was supposed to set up a Western shipbuilding yard in Indonesia, which would have been a bold and innovative move. This speculated expansion never occurred, however. The small Itoh outpost in Indonesia became Aritomo-san's place of exile.

The Case of the Waving Cat

That cat looks haughty

Sitting on his red cushion.

Shogun of the house.

"I must admit this case has me totally confused, Sensei."

Officer Suzuki's admission shocked and surprised me. He was not the kind of man that I would expect to ask for help, especially from a non-police officer. It actually increased my respect for him. It takes an intelligent man with a streak of humility to know when to ask for help.

"I was impressed by your ability to analyze what happened during the death of the Abbot," Officer Suzuki continued.

"But that was Sigerson-san," I protested. "I did almost nothing except translate for him. He made the observations and deductions that solved the case."

Officer Suzuki looked at me with a blank expression. He was too polite to contradict me but it was plain that it was inconceivable to him that a gaijin could show such exceptional abilities. Despite his intelligence, Officer Suzuki was a xenophobe and obviously had a low regard for foreigners. His posting at Karuizawa, with its large population of foreigners, must have been very difficult for him. I wondered what he did to upset someone enough to transfer him from Tokyo to Karuizawa.

"Of course, I would also like the help of the gaijin," Officer Suzuki said diplomatically. "But no matter who gives it, I need help because I am completely puzzled by the story that was told to me."

"Let me get Sigerson-san and you can tell us that story."

"Actually, while you get the gaijin I can go get the man who told me the puzzling story and you both can hear it directly."

We agreed to this and I went to fetch Sigerson-san. We returned to my office and in a few minutes Officer Suzuki and another man appeared. Officer Suzuki had obviously brought him with him when he came to seek my help.

The man was in his early forties, his hair was short, and he wore a rather common brown kimono. There was the ingratiating nature of the tradesman about him and he kept a smile plastered on his face and his head slightly bowed as Officer Suzuki introduced him.

"This is Akagi," Officer Suzuki said. "He owns a shop in the town that specializes in dried fish. I'll let him tell his story to you himself." I secretly congratulated myself for identifying Akagi's profession. Sigerson-san's methods were beginning to rub off on me a bit.

Akagi bowed. Some people might be a bit intimidated by being thrust center stage but in his occupation he was used to dealing with strangers and, despite his storekeeper's ways, he seemed eager to have a new audience for the tale he had to tell.

"Be sure to stop occasionally because I want to translate for my friend," I admonished Akagi.

"Huh? Oh, I see. You want the gaijin to know about what happened, too. All right, Sensei, I'll stop to let you translate." He cleared his throat.

"The trouble is that I am uncertain if he will return," he began. "I have bought a great number of cats and already spent a great amount of time, but if he doesn't return I will lose all that money."

I put up my hand. "Akagi, you must start at the beginning. We can't help you if we can't understand what happened, especially since you're talking about cats."

"I don't mean real cats," he said.

"What do you mean?"

"I mean *maneki neko*."

"Ah," I said. "Wait a minute while I explain to my friend." I told Sigerson-san that apparently the trouble had to do with maneki neko.

"Which are?"

"They're small statues of cats with one paw up, as if they are waving. You may have seen them in the shop windows in the town. They're used for good luck. They're supposed to invite customers into the store, which invites prosperity." Then I turned to Akagi. "Begin. But please start at the beginning and try to leave nothing out." I already knew how Sigerson-san liked to hear every detail of a story.

Akagi took a deep breath, then started once more.

"As the officer said, I run a shop in town that sells dried fish. It's a tough business because the gaijin population in Karuizawa doesn't eat much dried fish. Of course, we do a steady business with the Nihonjin, but it's not as good a business as you would expect from a town this size."

Akagi saw the expression on my face and decided to move on from the vicissitudes of the dried fish business and into his story.

"In any case, because business is so hard in this town I was very interested in the proposition that Ishibashi-san made to me."

"Don't jump ahead. Tell us who this Ishibashi-san is and how you met him and what his proposition was. Keep telling the story exactly as it happened," I prompted. Then I translated for Sigerson-san.

"As it happened?" Akagi asked.

"Yes. Step by step. And please try to relate any conversations, word for word," I said.

"Well, about three weeks ago I was cleaning up in preparation for closing my shop. I noticed a man walking by my shop window. He was about 35, dressed in a good kimono, and was someone I had never seen before. He wore a Western hat and had a Tokyo accent. As he passed the window of my shop he suddenly stopped, turned, and looked at the maneki neko I have in the window. He walked into my shop and stared at this maneki neko some more."

I held out my hand to stop him and translated for Sigerson-san.

"Ask him if there is anything special about this cat statue," Sigerson-san said.

Akagi shook his head. "As far as I know it's a common maneki neko. But that's not what the man told me. He seemed quite excited about my statue. I asked him if I could do anything for him and he said to me that I could tell him some more about my maneki neko. I thought he must be some kind of lunatic and I told him that I didn't know anything about the statue and that I would have to ask him to leave my shop because I was closing it down. My wife was in the shop with me and she said that we should perhaps ask the gentleman why he wants to know about the statue.

"The man said his name was Ishibashi Toshimichi, and that he was a member of the cult of the maneki neko. I've never heard of such a cult, but Japan is a big country with many religious groups." Akagi shrugged, as if to say he had no interest in the ecumenical religious taste of our country.

"Ishibashi-san said that his excitement over my maneki neko must seem strange. But, he added, he thought the maneki neko in my shop window is actually a rather rare one. He looked at the bottom of the statue and said he was right. It was produced at a small factory in Saitama, and that only a limited number of them were made before the factory went out of business. I got excited about this and asked Ishibashi-san if the statue was valuable. He shook his head sadly and said it wasn't. That was a great disappointment to me. As I said, the dried fish business is tough in this town. But, he added, the fact that I had such a rare maneki neko in my window might turn out to be my lucky day anyway.

"I asked him what he meant and he asked me if I knew anything about the cult of the maneki neko. I said no, so he asked if I knew the true meaning of the maneki neko. Of course I said it was to invite customers into my shop so they would buy something. Ishibashi-san shook his head and said this was what most merchants thought because they don't know the origins of the maneki neko. He then said he would tell me the true story, and at the end it would prove to my financial interest if I listened to the story closely. To be truthful I wasn't too interested in learning the story behind my ceramic cat, but the promise of financial reward caught my attention.

"Many years ago, Ishibashi-san said, Lord Ii, who was a key retainer of the Shogun, was walking in the forest near Setagaya. A heavy rain suddenly sprang up and Lord Ii took shelter under the branches of a large tree. As he stood there waiting for the rain to stop he spied a small temple hidden in the forest. Sitting in the door of the temple was a calico cat. The cat appeared to be waving vigorously to Lord Ii, inviting him to leave the tree and come to the temple.

"The Lord was relatively dry under the tree so he was reluctant to enter the heavy rain to heed the summons of a cat. Still, the cat seemed so insistent and so human-like with its waving that finally Lord Ii thought the strange behavior of the cat was a sign from heaven and that he should obey it.

"So, despite the rain, Lord Ii ran to the temple, getting quite soaked in the process. As he reached the temple the cat stopped waving and simply sat looking up at the Lord, acting like a normal cat. Lord Ii felt both foolish and annoyed at this incident, thinking he had misinterpreted the strange gestures of the cat, getting wet for no good reason.

"Just then there was a tremendous explosion behind the Lord. Lord Ii spun around just in time to see a huge lightning bolt striking the tree he had stood under. The bolt was so powerful it shattered the tree and the heavy trunk of the tree came crashing to the earth in the exact spot he had been standing just moments before. It would certainly have killed him.

"Lord Ii was so grateful he looked for the owner of the cat. The owner turned out to be a humble priest who maintained the temple. The priest vowed that the cat was simply a normal cat and he had never seen her do anything like waving at a passerby. As Lord Ii talked to the priest he realized that he had found a learned man who was wise about both religion and life. Lord Ii started visiting the temple, which is Gotokuji temple in the Setagaya neighborhood of Tokyo.

"The Lord was so impressed with the knowledge of the priest, and so grateful about being saved by the intervention of the cat, that he endowed the temple with many gifts, making it prosperous. This allowed the priest to show his gratitude by feeding and pampering the cat. The cat had a good and happy life for many years, despite the fact that it never again exhibited strange behavior, such as waving to people.

"When the cat died the priest buried it at Gotokuji, erecting a headstone that showed an image of the waving cat. One can go to the temple to this day and see this headstone and the cat image carved on it. This is where we get our image for the maneki neko.

"Most merchants think it is simply a symbol of good luck, enticing patrons into their shop. But from this story you can see that a maneki neko is actually a benevolent figure, protecting people from bad fortune. In a way, it is like a Kannon, the Goddess of Mercy, and you should respect a maneki neko statue the same way you would respect a statue of the Kannon.

"I expressed my surprise at this story," Akagi said. "I didn't know the true story of the maneki neko. Ishibashi-san told me that most people don't know about it, which is why the cult of the maneki neko was formed.

"My wife then said to Ishibashi-san that he said that the maneki neko would bring good luck to our household and that the story of the waving cat would result in our financial advantage.

"Ishibashi-san smiled at us and said that the maneki neko would bring good fortune to us. He looked at me and told me he would pay me to visit every shopkeeper in the surrounding area. If the shop didn't have a maneki neko in the window I was supposed to give them one. In addition, I must tell every shopkeeper the true story of the maneki neko, just as Ishibashi-san told it to me.

"But how can I do that, I asked him, because I have to run my shop?

"You could do it in the evening, my wife suggested. She said she would close the shop down and prepare dinner for us as I visited the other shops in the Karuizawa area, telling the wonderful story of the maneki neko.

"Ishibashi-san said that would be satisfactory but he wanted me to spend at least two hours every evening doing this. He said this was a key point. He said he would check on me to make sure I was doing this because the cult wanted the story of the maneki neko told faithfully and fully by the people they employ. He said he wanted me to start the next evening and that he would come back in a week to pay me fifty Yen plus the cost of any maneki neko statues I gave out. With that, Ishibashi-san said goodbye and left."

"And why have you come to Officer Suzuki about this?" I asked.

"Because it has been nine days and Ishibashi-san never returned. I have been swindled in some way! I want the police to get me my money," he said simply.

"Yes, you want the help of the police but you were so anxious to make money that you didn't even bother to find out where the man was staying!" Officer Suzuki said with scorn. Using Sigerson-san's methods, from this I was able to deduce that Officer Suzuki probably came from a samurai family. He had the samurai's contempt for the merchant.

I looked at Sigerson-san and asked, "Do you have any questions?"

"Just two," Sigerson-san said. "First, where did you meet your wife?"

"My wife?" Akagi asked.

"That's what Sigerson-san asked," I responded.

"I met her in the Tsukiji district in Tokyo, where the big fish market is. I go there periodically to buy dried fish from the vendors in that district. But what does this have to do with this whole waving cat business?"

I told Sigerson-san this. He nodded and said, "I will explain things later. My second question is, what does he normally have for dinner?"

I was surprised by Sigerson-san's first question and astounded by his second. However, I had seen the efficacy of his unusual methods and passed the question on to Akagi.

"Why does he want to know that?" Officer Suzuki said. He was as mystified as Akagi and me over what Sigerson-san wanted to know.

"I don't know," I answered, "but he will not explain his thought process until everything is settled in his mind. I know these are unusual questions, Akagi, but if you could answer his questions I am sure it will lead to a solution to this problem."

Akagi shrugged and said, "Normally I eat a simple supper. Usually some rice left over from breakfast, some pickles and some dried fish. I will appreciate the gaijin-sama's help, but these questions are very strange," he added.

I translated the first part of his response for Sigerson-san and left out Akagi's comment. Sigerson-san seemed very satisfied with the answers he got. He sat back in his chair and said, "Please tell Mr. Akagi that he should continue his proselytizing for the cult of the waving cat until the man returns. And please tell Officer Suzuki to return here tomorrow and I will be able to provide him with more information about this unusual situation."

"Tomorrow?"

"Yes. I simply need to confirm a few things but it's obvious what is occurring."

"Well, it isn't obvious to me," I said.

Sigerson-san gave me that fleeting smile of his, but didn't enlighten me on what was so obvious to him. That was a bit infuriating, but I was learning that Sigerson-san would eventually explain when his deductions were confirmed and I just had to be patient. Indeed, since I was not as good at drawing deductions from scanty facts as Sigerson-san, I had no choice but to be patient as he finished his investigations.

I relayed the message to Akagi and Officer Suzuki that Sigerson-san would have information for them the next day. Both seemed surprised that Sigerson-san would have information so quickly and both said they would do as requested.

After my office hours that day Sigerson-san asked me if we could take a walk into town. "I would like to see Mr. Akagi's shop," he said.

We strolled from my house to downtown Karuizawa and soon found Akagi's shop. It was a typical, modest two-story wooden affair with the store on the bottom story and living quarters above. In front of the shop was a carved wooden fish so customers who couldn't read would know what was sold within. The dried fish shop was flanked on one side by a greengrocer and on the other side was a curiosity shop.

After a glance, Sigerson-san said, "I've seen all I need to, Doctor, but I would like to look at the curiosity shop."

I walked Sigerson-san over to the curiosity shop and stood in front enjoying the air as he went inside. He seemed to be browsing, looking at the various items in the shop.

"Sensei! Sensei!" I winced at the sound of that voice and silently cursed that I didn't follow Sigerson-san into the curiosity shop. I sighed and turned around.

There was Takada-san hurrying down the street towards me, pulling a lanky young girl after her.

"Sensei! How lucky of us to meet you here in the town!" She shoved the girl forward. "This is my daughter, Naomi," Takada-san announced. Naomi-chan looked both embarrassed and ungainly. I failed to see why Takada-san thought Naomi-chan would be a good match for me, and Naomi-chan, who was meeting me for the first time, didn't seem lovestruck, either. More importantly, I was not prepared to marry again. Indeed, I might never be. It seemed that it was Takada-san who, for whatever reason, was determined to have me as a son-in-law.

"Hello, it's a pleasure to meet you," I said. "*Hajimemashite.*" I tried to be neutral but I was severely vexed by Takada-san's uncouthness. Why couldn't she hire a *nakoudo*, a matchmaker, like any other civilized person? That way I could politely refuse the suggestion of a marriage with her daughter to the nakoudo and all of us would be spared awkward situations. Instead, Takada-san's pushiness and, dare I say it, obsession with arranging a match between myself and her daughter was acutely embarrassing and uncomfortable.

Naomi-chan, Takada-san's daughter, seemed to be aware of her mother's inappropriate forwardness because she seemed genuinely reluctant to have her mother push this introduction. She gave a bow to me and awkwardly studied the ground in front of her.

"Say hello, Naomi!" Takada-san ordered.

Naomi-chan bowed again and said, "Good afternoon, Sensei," in a weak voice. This time she gave a deep bow. It was excessively deep and I took the bow as an apology for her mother's behavior. I felt sorry for Naomi-chan.

An awkward silence ensued. Takada-san poked her daughter and said, "Say something more!"

"I'm sorry that you lost your wife," Naomi-chan said. "When she visited us I thought she was really a wonderful and sweet person."

"Thank you for your kind words," I replied, anxious to extricate myself from this awkward situation. I noticed that Sigerson-san was at the shop's counter purchasing something and I excused myself to enter the shop. As I took my leave I could hear Takada-san sharply criticizing her daughter for not taking advantage of this chance meeting more fully. This made me feel even more sorry for Naomi-chan.

In the shop I joined Sigerson-san at the counter and promptly asked the shopkeeper to give him the nihonjin price instead of the tourist gaijin price. The shopkeeper wasn't happy about reducing the price but he complied. When I saw what Sigerson-san was buying I was quite astonished. It was a pair of silk slippers. They looked like they were made in China, but they were of the design the English call a Persian slipper.

When Sigerson-san finished paying I asked him, "Why do you want those? They can't possibly fit your feet."

"I don't intend to use them on my feet," he said. "In fact, I intend to throw one slipper away and only use its mate."

"Whatever for?"

"I intend to put my pipe tobacco in it," he said.

I have been astounded by many things gaijin do, but this one caused an emotion beyond surprise. The idea of placing your pipe tobacco into an old used Persian slipper that strangers have worn on their dirty feet went beyond the strange and into the perverse. The thought of smoking such tainted tobacco caused me to gag. Still, my time in England taught me that despite their outward propriety, English can engage in some very strange activities when in private. Of course, I made no mention of my aversion to Sigerson-san's plans for the slipper. He was a guest, but this strange act was pushing the boundaries of tolerance for a guest!

"Now, doctor, I suggest we stroll around the block and then go to the Mampei Hotel for some food. We will have to wait until this evening to complete the rest of our investigation."

I walked with him around the block where Akagi had his shop. I saw absolutely nothing unusual and I couldn't understand Sigerson-san's desire for a stroll. Then we went to the Mampei and enjoyed a pleasant early dinner.

After dinner we walked back to Akagi's shop and took a position where we could watch the shop unnoticed. I had never done this kind of spying before and it made me nervous and uncomfortable, but Sigerson-san seemed perfectly at ease about our secret observations.

At sundown Akagi left his shop. Tucked under one arm was a cheap maneki neko doll, so I assumed he was leaving to go proselytize about the true meaning of the waving cat. I thought we were going to follow Akagi and started to walk after him, but Sigerson-san placed a hand on my arm, indicating that we should wait.

Inside Akagi's shop I could see his wife hurrying to clean up things to close the shop. She quickly covered the counters with cloth and extinguished the lamps. Sigerson-san pointed down the street and I saw a man furtively walking towards the shop. He wore a kimono and a western hat. Then, to my great surprise, the man quickly opened the door of the darkened shop and slipped inside. After a few moments lamplight could be seen in a window on the upper floor of the shop. It did not require a sordid mind to guess what was transpiring in that room.

Sigerson-san made no comment and had no reaction to these surprising events. Or perhaps I should say the events were surprising to me. Sigerson-san had apparently already deduced they were about to occur. After a bit more than an hour the man slipped out of the shop and made his way down the street. He seemed to be in a good mood and walked with the swagger I identify as *Ginbura*, that distinctive stroll identified with people from Tokyo. I was sure it was Ishibashi-san, the maneki neko man. We followed him at a discreet distance.

Ishibashi-san went to a *ryokan* located near the outskirts of town and entered. He did not notice he was followed by Sigerson-san and me.

"Do you know the name of that establishment?" Sigerson-san asked me.

"Yes, it's a traditional Japanese inn called the Wind on Pine Tree Mountain, *Kaze Matsuyama*."

"Good," Sigerson-san said with satisfaction. "That wraps everything up rather neatly. If you can ask Officer Suzuki to visit us alone tomorrow I will explain it to him."

I was waiting for him to explain it to me, too, but as usual Sigerson-san was not about to reveal his thinking in small portions. He wanted to wait until he could serve the entire banquet, from beginning to end.

The next morning Officer Suzuki, Sigerson-san, and I met in the parlor of my home. It was finally time for the feast.

"Religious groups don't hire people to proselytize," Sigerson-san started. "They want true believers to spread their message. That is why missionaries from England and elsewhere come to Japan. It would be ridiculous to send someone half-way around the world to spread a religious message if a church could simply hire a non-believing local to do it. Therefore, from the beginning of Mr. Akagi's story, it was obvious that the cult of the waving cat was simply a ruse to get Mr. Akagi out of his shop.

"What was more than suggestive in this case, however, was the fact that Ishibashi seemed only interested in getting Mr. Akagi away from his shop. He made no attempt to get Mrs. Akagi away, too. In fact, it was Mrs. Akagi who urged her husband to listen to and participate in the effort to proselytize the bogus religion. I wanted to confirm my suspicions, however, and yesterday Dr. Watanabe and I went to the Akagi shop to observe it.

"The Akagi's dried fish shop was not adjacent to anything of note, such as a bank or jewelry store. If the Akagi shop were next to another business of high value, such as a jeweler, there was the possibility that a burglary was being planned, perhaps by digging a tunnel or breaking through an adjoining wall. We circled the entire block and there was not a business of note beside or behind the Akagi shop. Therefore, it was obvious the object of interest to Ishibashi was something—or someone—inside the Akagi shop, not the shop building.

"If you'll recall, I asked Mr. Akagi where he met his wife. He said from a district in Tokyo. When you talk to Ishibashi, Officer Suzuki, I think you will find that he comes from the same district in Tokyo and he knew Mrs. Akagi before she got married."

When I translated this part, Officer Suzuki asked, "But why did he ask Akagi what kind of dinner he ate?"

"Because if he had an elaborate dinner it would indicate that Mrs. Akagi didn't have time to be indiscreet," Sigerson-san said. "The dinner Akagi described would only take a few minutes to throw together.

"By the way," Sigerson-san continued, "You can find Ishibashi at the Japanese inn called the Wind on Pine Mountain. He won't be registered as Ishibashi there, but it should be easy enough to identify him."

"But has Ishibashi actually committed a crime?" Officer Suzuki asked. "Assuming Ishibashi actually pays Akagi what he promised him, should I tell Akagi about his wife's affair? Isn't this a private matter?"

Sigerson-san smiled. "For the first time since I arrived in this country I am happy that I am blissfully ignorant of your language and customs. That, gentlemen, is a problem that I will leave you to solve."

The Adventure of the Battleship Plans

Sheet of large paper

Covered with lines and numbers.

Worth a human life?

"This is a most serious crisis, perhaps the most serious we have faced in Japan. That is the reason I have called for your help." Hugh Fraser, Envoy Extraordinary and Minister Plenipotentiary, and head of the British Legation, leaned forward in his chair. "The instructions we received from the Foreign Office said we were to facilitate your stay in Japan and keep you incognito, but the instructions also said that if a crisis presented itself, we could use your talents to help us. We now need those talents."

Less than half an hour before, Sigerson-san had received a note from Col. Ashworth asking for an immediate meeting. The Colonel had sent a jinrikisha to pick up Sigerson-san and his note stressed the urgency of meeting. Therefore I was a bit surprised when Sigerson-san asked me if I could go with him to the meeting.

"Are you sure?" I asked.

"Of course, my dear Doctor Watanabe. You have been invaluable with the adventures we've had during my stay here. After all, I do not speak or read the language and your knowledge of local customs and English are the only things that allow me to function in this environment. I do not know what Col. Ashworth wants, but obviously it is something that has to do with Japan so I will certainly need you, if you can spare me the time."

"Of course," I responded and within minutes we

were jammed into the jinrikisha and on our way to Col. Ashworth's summer house in Karuizawa.

Once at the house we were immediately shown to the Colonel's study. There we found the Colonel and a gentleman. They both looked surprised by my presence and I immediately felt uncomfortable for accepting Sigerson-san's invitation. The man identified himself as Mr. Fraser, but even before that I recognized his face from an illustration in the *Tokyo Shimbun* and knew he was Hugh Fraser, the head of the British Legation in Japan.

"I must confess that I am a bit surprised that two of you came. What I have to discuss with you is extremely confidential in nature and I had hoped to talk to you privately, Mister... ah... Sigerson."

"Come now, Minister Fraser," Sigerson-san said, ignoring the Minister's effort to keep incognito. "There is no need to hide anything from Doctor Watanabe. He has proven to be a trustworthy companion and friend. More importantly, he is invaluable in any investigations you want me to make here. Indeed, he is essential."

The Minister and the Colonel looked at each other for a moment, then the Minister said, "I meant no offense to the Doctor and I must admit that it would be foolish of me to ask for help and then not trust your judgment about who else will be necessary to give that help. I apologize, Doctor."

"No apologies are necessary," I said. The Minister seemed surprised by my English. I admit I have a good aptitude for the English language, but gaijin just naturally assume that any Japanese will speak English with a thick accent, ignoring the fact that just a decade ago the Japanese government was discussing the possibility of making English the official language of Japan. Of course, we Japanese have the same surprise when we meet a gaijin who can speak good Nihongo, too.

"We have a crisis," the Minister repeated.

"And what is this crisis?" Sigerson-san asked.

"As you may know, the Japanese government has chosen to model many of its modern institutions on various European countries. The police are organized on the French model, the Army is structured like the German army, the lower-schools are organized on an American model, and the Japanese Foreign Office and Navy are organized on the British model.

"Because of the close relationship between Her Majesty's government and the government of the Emperor, we have sold Japan several warships. Most of these ships are refurbished vessels that are no longer top ships-of-the-line in European waters, but are still powerful in Asian waters. Recently, however, we have agreed to provide Japan with several examples of our most modern battleships.

"These vessels incorporate all the knowledge we have acquired in the two decades since the launching of the HMS Royal Sovereign. They will be the most powerful warships in Asia. We have held back nothing in the design of these ships. In other words, they are the most advanced and powerful warships in the world and are matched only by the battleships in Her Majesty's own Navy.

"As part of the preparations for building these ships we recently sent a copy of the blueprints for the first vessel to the Imperial Japanese Navy. The Japanese have representatives in England, of course, but the Naval Headquarters wanted the Japanese to acquaint themselves with the operational and maintenance issues these powerful warships will require, and having copies of the blueprints will facilitate that.

"The plans arrived in Japan just a week ago. They were in the possession of Captain Reginald Norman. He and an escort left the cruiser HMS Invecta in Yokohama harbor on their way to the Japanese Imperial Navy Headquarters. The entire party took individual jinrikisha and started toward the Headquarters but before they left the dock area the jinrikisha holding Captain Norman suddenly turned into a side street. Despite the yelling of the rest of the party, the other jinrikisha would not stop and the other officers in the party had to actually jump out of the moving carriages. They ran to the side street but could not find any evidence of Captain Norman. Two days later the body of Captain Norman was found floating in Yokohama harbor. His throat had been cut."

"And the battleship plans, which Captain Norman undoubtedly had in the jinrikisha with him, were gone," Sigerson-san said.

Minister Fraser looked a little startled by Sigerson-san's rapid deduction regarding the plans but even I was able to comprehend that the late Captain Norman must have had the battleship plans with him.

"That's correct," the Minister said, "and the theft of the plans has caused consternation in the British Legation and a frenzy amongst our Japanese friends."

"Who would want these plans?" Sigerson-san asked.

"Since they represent the latest thinking of the British Navy, any seafaring country in the world would be interested. We are the undisputed leader in battleship design. I dare say the Americans would love to get a look at those plans, although I don't think they would go so far as murder to get them."

"Who would go that far?" Sigerson-san said.

"Because of the rising tensions between Japan and China, the Chinese would, especially if war breaks out. The Kaiser is of course building a Navy designed to challenge Britain's domination of the seas so the Germans would want those plans badly enough to kill for them. The Russians are also candidates because they potentially face both the British and Japanese navies in Pacific or European waters. Those plans would give them valuable information on two possible enemies.

"Because of the chance of war the Chinese Legation is not free to roam the country," Minister Fraser continued, "but we think it is significant that members of both the Russian Legation and the German Legation will arrive in Karuizawa on today's train. Moreover, we have been told that both representatives have taken rooms at the Mampei Hotel."

A long silence filled the room. Col. Ashworth cleared his throat and said, "Of course, it could be a coincidence…"

Both Minister Fraser and Sigerson-san gave the Colonel looks that strangled his comment before it was completely formed. I was very fond of the Colonel but even an amateur in these matters, such as me, could see that the confluence of events precluded coincidence as the cause for members of both the Russian and German Legations appearing at Karuizawa on the same day and staying at the same hotel. It was probable that they were not just here to take in the mountain air.

"One thing I don't understand," the Colonel said, taking a new tack, "is why both the Germans and the Russians should appear at Karuizawa. Surely if one of them had the plans they would want to get them out of the country."

"Obviously they don't have the plans," Sigerson-san said. "This crime has all the earmarks of a crime syndicate that used to be led by a man called the Napoleon of Crime, Professor Moriarty. Only his organization could know when the battleship plans were being transported to Japan. Even in this country, as far removed from Europe as you can get, his organization was able to arrange a theft and murder to obtain the plans. In addition, his agents certainly have the contacts to negotiate with the Germans and Russians to sell them the plans. I deduce that the reason both the Germans and Russians are here is because this crime organization is selling the plans to the highest bidder and they will hold an auction right here in Karuizawa."

Col. Ashworth listened to this with growing alarm. "Great Heavens, sir, where is this Napoleon of Crime?"

Sigerson-san smiled grimly. "He is dead now. But this theft is undoubtedly a crime planned by this evil genius before his demise. The question now is how we can thwart his plan and recover the battleship plans."

Minister Fraser looked thoughtful. "I agree we must focus on getting those plans back. However, I know more about the circumstances that brought you to Japan than the Colonel, Mr. Sigerson, and I must withdraw my request for help from you. I shan't get you involved in this affair if Professor Moriarty's organization is involved. It would put you in mortal danger and potentially reveal your presence here in Japan."

"I appreciate your concern, but this is a matter of national importance to two nations, England and Japan. Under these circumstances my personal safety is of no consequence," Sigerson-san said. Needless to say, by this time my head was reeling from the conversation I was privy to.

The Minister shook his head. "I'm sorry, sir, but my orders from the Foreign Office were quite explicit. The British Legation in Japan was to keep you incognito and, at all hazards, keep you safe. I would hardly be doing either if I exposed you to a ruthless criminal organization that undoubtedly would seek revenge if it knew you were in Japan."

"Upon my word," Col. Ashworth said, "who are

you, Mr. Sigerson?"

"Colonel, Mr. Sigerson is a Norwegian explorer," the Minister said in a voice that was obviously designed to silence the Colonel.

I cleared my throat. "I know I am only here at Sigerson-san's insistence and I obviously don't understand all that is happening but I have a proposal that may be useful."

The three men looked at me in surprise but Sigerson-san said, "By all means, please tell us your proposal, Doctor."

Encouraged, I continued. "As I understand it, Sigerson-san is in Japan to remain incognito. Unfortunately, he believes the perpetrators of this recent crime are the very people that Minister Fraser says he is trying to avoid. In the relatively short time I have known him I have witnessed Sigerson-san's amazing powers when it comes to unraveling crimes. I can see why you would want Sigerson-san's help in retrieving the plans. In fact, I think Sigerson-san missed his calling and should have been a policeman or detective instead of an explorer." That last remark brought an enigmatic smile to Sigerson-san's lips.

"While he has been in Japan I have acted as Sigerson-san's voice because he does not speak Japanese," I said. "In this instance, I propose that I act as his eyes and ears, too. I can keep my surgery hours to a minimum and can spend considerable time at the Mampei Hotel. I will make observations and relay to Sigerson-san what I have seen and heard. He can then form any deductions he might and confer with you gentlemen about what to do. It will not be as efficient as Sigerson-san going to the Mampei himself but it will isolate him from who might have an interest in knowing he is in Japan."

The Minister was shaking his head even before I finished with my proposal. "I'm sorry, Doctor," he said, "but there is far too much danger involved for you to get involved with this situation."

"Mr. Minister," I said, "I fully understand the risks. Whoever stole the battleship plans had no hesitation to kill a British officer to obtain them. I have no illusions that they will not hesitate to kill anyone who is intent on retrieving those plans, including a humble country doctor. However, I recognize that the interests of Japan are at stake in this matter. Those plans are rightfully the property of my country's government and the theft of the plans and the accompanying murder occurred here in Japan. Mr. Minister, you and the Colonel are loyal to your Queen and country and are willing to risk your life in service to that loyalty. You are even asking the help of Sigerson-san, who is Norwegian and not a British subject. Just as you are loyal to your Queen, I am no less loyal to my Emperor and my country and I am no less willing to risk my life to express that loyalty."

There was silence in the room after my little speech. Finally Minister Fraser looked at Sigerson-san and said, "What do you think?"

"I think the Doctor has been invaluable to me during my stay in Japan regarding several matters. I have no reason to believe he will not be equally valuable in this matter."

Of course I kept a serious expression on my face, as befit the situation and the presence of the Minister, but inside I was smiling. I had respect for Sigerson-san and was happy to see he considered my humble contributions to our adventures together as useful.

The Minister sighed. After a moment's hesitation he said, "All right. Beggars can't be choosers and in this case we are certainly begging for help. Doctor, we welcome your help and I hope for the sake of both our countries that we are all successful at recovering those plans."

We spent a few more minutes deciding how we would arrange to watch the members of the German and Russian Legations at the Mampei, guided by Sigerson-san's advice.

When we were done planning Sigerson-san said, "The thieves will want to sell the plans for the highest price, which is why I believe some form of auction will take place. We must be alert to discover how and where this auction will be held. We must keep focused over the next few days."

On that somber note we all went to our posts. Sigerson-san was to stay at the Colonel's house with Minister Fraser. The Colonel's house would act as our command post and receive any messages that might arrive from Tokyo or Yokohama about developments there. Col. Ashworth was to act as the liaison between myself and Sigerson-san and the Minister, and I was to watch at the Mampei.

Once at the Mampei I sat in a comfortable lobby seat where I could command a view of the entrance and the registration desk and settled down. I picked up one of the copies of *Punch Magazine* that the Mampei had for the reading pleasure of its English guests. The issue I looked at was months old, as were all the English magazines and newspapers, because of the shipping time from England. It didn't matter. I was obviously not there to spend a pleasant day at the hotel but to watch the movements of the Russian and German Legation members staying at the hotel. Besides, I did not understand most of the English humor in *Punch*. I understood the words, mind you, but not the humor.

As I sat perusing the magazine a smartly groomed Japanese in a Western style suit came up to me. "Excuse me, sir," he said, "but aren't you Doctor Watanabe?"

I looked up. "Yes I am."

"I'm sorry to bother you Doctor but I would like to introduce myself. I am Kurihara, the new Assistant Manager of the Mampei Hotel." He bowed to me in the formal manner, with a stiff back.

I immediately stood and bowed back, although it was naturally less formal and certainly not as deep. "I am glad to meet you," I said. "I hope you don't mind my spending a few days here at the hotel without checking in. My house is having some repairs done to it and I am bothered by the noise."

"Doctor, you are always welcome at this establishment. You are the doctor to most of the foreign community and also the personal physician to Lord Itoh. We are honored to have you here."

I waved my hand in a suitable display of modesty. "I am only the physician to Lord Itoh when he is at his villa in Karuizawa," I said.

"But both he and Itoh-sama sing your praises. That is why I have approached you. I know you are here to relax but we have a guest who is a bit ill. Could you take the time to see him?"

"Who is it?"

"Major Staudinger," Kurihara-san said. "He is a member of the German Legation who is spending a few days with us. He checked in just before you arrived but unfortunately he has a high fever and is very ill. I know it is a great imposition but perhaps you can see him? The Hotel does not yet have a house physician and it would be a true kindness if you could see the Major. We are worried about his condition."

I couldn't believe my luck. I was sent to observe the Russian and German Legation members at the Mampei and now I had a chance to meet the German directly. "Of course I'll see Major Staudinger," I readily agreed.

Kurihara-san took me into the hotel and up a flight of stairs. He stopped at a door and knocked softly.

"*Ja*? Yes? Who is there?" The man's voice was raspy and weak.

"It's Kurihara, the Assistant Manager of the hotel. I've brought a doctor to see you," he said in passable English. It struck me as strange that both Kurihara and the Major were conversing in English, a language not native to either of them.

I could hear a man moving in the room, then the sound of the key turning in the door. The door opened and a thin, handsome man was standing before me. He had short black hair and his face was flushed red with fever. He opened the door for us and wobbled back to the bed. Kurihara-san and I entered, closing the door behind us.

I examined the Major and quickly determined that he was suffering from a bad cold. "Make sure that he gets plenty of fluids," I told Kurihara-san, "things like soup and tea." Then I turned to the Major and said, "If you rest a few days and take plenty of liquids you will soon recover. You have a cold. I don't think it's anything more serious, but it's imperative that you stay in bed and rest."

"No, no. I have some business to accomplish here. I must be able to get up." Major Staudinger tried to sit up but he was in such a weakened state that he soon collapsed back on the bed. When he came to open the door it must have drained him of all reserves of energy.

"I think you can see now that my advice is sound, Major Staudinger," I said. "Are you new to Japan?"

He nodded weakly.

"For some reason colds seem to be more serious when gaijin first come here," I said, "but next year you will be able to bear them as if you were in Europe. I had the same experience the first year I went to England but I soon adjusted. I know it feels as though you are suffering from something more serious but I assure you it is just a cold. With rest you will be better." I looked at Kurihara-san and asked, "Can you arrange to have Major Staudinger's meals brought to his room for the next couple of days?"

"Of course," Kurihara-san said.

"Good. I will write a list of recommended foods. It will be mostly soup and bread, but make sure the Major also has plenty of fresh water because he is running a fever. As I told you, I will be spending some time at the hotel during the day and evening, so I will be available for follow-up examinations." I looked to the Major. "Do you have any questions?" I asked him.

"No. Thank you for your kindness, Doctor," he said in a weak voice.

"Nonsense. Please just rest and get well. I'll look in on you later to make sure you are resting."

Kurihara-san and I let ourselves out of the Major's room.

"Thank you, Doctor," Kurihara-san said to me. "I was very worried about the Major because he looked so ill when he checked in."

"It is strange to go on vacation with such a bad cold," I said. "But he did say he had some business to attend to. Do you know anything about that?" I probed.

Kurihara-san looked puzzled. "I'm afraid not. The Major didn't share his plans with the staff. After he's rested I'll ask if there's anything we can do to help facilitate his business."

I doubted the Major would be asking for help in the business he was in Karuizawa for. I immediately went to the lobby and asked for some paper and ink. "Do you want a Japanese brush or a Western pen?" Kurihara-san asked.

"I have a pen with me," I said. "I'll write a menu suitable for the Major during his convalescence."

"Of course, Doctor. Just inform the front desk when your menu is done and I'll see it's followed faithfully."

I quickly wrote my menu and gave it to the front desk. Then I took another piece of paper from the writing desk in the lobby and quickly wrote a note of a different sort.

Sigerson-san,

Major Staudinger, from the German Legation, is ill. He will have to stay at the Mampei for at least two days. I am attending to him. Should I use this opportunity to do more than observe the various guests and report about them to you?

- Watanabe

Just as I finished my note someone entered the Mampei to check in. It was a gaijin man in a well-tailored blue suit. He was in his early fifties, he had a stocky build, and he wore a large mustache and a sharply pointed beard.

"I am Count Kirovsky," he announced to the desk clerk. "You have a reservation for me."

"Yes sir." Kurihara-san stepped in to check in such an important visitor. "The Russian Legation made the reservation. Do you need quarters for servants, too?"

Count Kirovsky waved his hand. "No, no. I am traveling incognito so I am here alone. Send someone to the station for my luggage," he said imperiously.

"Of course, sir," Kurihara-san said. "Let me show you to your suite and then I will attend to your luggage."

Kurihara-san kept an impassive face but I was amused that the Count, after announcing his name and title so grandly, should also assert that he was traveling incognito. When I got a chance, I vowed to check the English dictionary in my library to assure that I was correct in my understanding of the word incognito.

I took my note and walked into the Mampei's bar. As I expected, sitting at a table in the corner was Col. Ashworth, reading one of the old *Punch* magazines and nursing a gin and tonic. I walked over to him and greeted him. I sat next to him and made some small talk. At the same time I surreptitiously handed him my note. Within a few minutes he excused himself and left to deliver my note to the Minister and Sigerson-san. This was as we had agreed to but I must say this skulking about made me feel a bit foolish. I thought about the British Naval Officer with his throat slit and the farcical elements of this secrecy suddenly didn't seem excessive.

When I returned to the lobby another guest was checking in.

A large red-headed woman stomped into the hotel. The European women who form the clientele of the Mampei were of the better class. By that I mean they are properly coiffed and they are properly dressed in custom fitted European dresses. This woman was neither.

Her stout body was dressed in a strange combination, even for a gaijin. She was wearing a man's shirt, some kind of voluminous gray skirt, and brown riding boots. We often have Christian missionaries head for the remote parts of Japan, sometimes on foot, sometimes on bicycle. They are almost always dressed in a costume more suited for shopping in Yokohama than wandering the countryside of Tohoku or some other remote place in our country. The men are often in suits and the women always wear dresses. I have never seen a gaijin woman dressed as this one was, although the outfit was admirably practical for wandering in remote areas.

The woman's curly red hair was peeking out from under a man's tan hat. What I could see of her hair was frizzy and flying in all directions. Framed by this hair was a round puffy face, burnt raw and red by wind and sun. Frankly, she looked very much like a *saru*.

Of course it is impolite to compare a woman to a monkey but with her red face, wild reddish hair, and scowling expression, that is just what she looked like. From my time in England I knew the English felt free in expressing the most unflattering comments about people from other places. These comments were most often heard about people from Asia or Africa, but they were also frequently made about other Europeans, especially the French and Germans. I was never sure if this free expression of unflattering national comments was an acceptable part of English culture but I heard them from people of all classes, including the better classes. We Japanese, perhaps because we are also an island people, often harbor similar opinions of gaijin; we just don't usually express them so freely.

"I am Elizabeth Trees and I require a room," the red-headed woman announced imperiously.

The desk clerk, who was used to dealing with gaijin, seemed totally unfazed by her demand. "Yes Madam..."

"Miss!" the woman corrected sharply.

"... ah, Miss, of course. Pardon me. We are happy to accommodate you." He turned the registry book to face her and provided Miss Trees with a pen.

Before she signed, Miss Trees looked out the front

door of the hotel and motioned. Four bedraggled porters came through the door, each one staggering under a huge load. They hauled a collection of trunks and large canvas bags. Each looked like he had walked to the Mampei across some considerable distance, not just hauled things from the railroad station.

The front desk clerk quickly rang a bell several times and several bellmen appeared in the lobby. The hotel staff took in the situation and went to the porters and relieved them of their load. There was an amusing aspect to this that made me smile, especially when I noticed that one of the boxes that Miss Trees hauled with her was labeled "Barlows Patent Rubberized Folding Bathtub." Bringing a bathtub to Japan was like (what is it the English say?) bringing coals to Newcastle!

"We meet here in two days. Understand?" Miss Trees said to her porters in English. One of the porters nodded and informed the other three in Japanese what her instructions were. "Ask her for payment," one of them said in Japanese, "then we can go back to our village." The one who spoke a little English said, "I don't know how to ask that. Besides, I'm afraid she will get mad again. This is truly a scary woman!" I chuckled to myself at this but the porters weren't smiling. Perhaps they truly were frightened of the formidable Miss Trees.

As the bellmen from the Mampei lugged all Miss Trees's luggage up to her room I reflected that there was plenty of room to secrete a large roll of battleship plans in the trunks or the many boxes and bags she traveled with.

Of course, a woman stealing the battleship plans would go against all expectations of society. In my opinion that is what would make it highly successful. If one thinks a woman is not capable of ruthlessness to achieve her goals then one has not studied history closely.

As I considered the likelihood that Miss Trees was

the holder of the battleship plans another guest entered the lobby. He was a thin man dressed in a black coat. He would have been tall but age had bent him over and he shuffled to the desk with a distinct limp. He wore colored glasses and his face was turned down because the light seemed to bother his eyes. Wisps of stray gray hair appeared from under his black hat, although I noticed his large hands did not appear to be those of a terribly old man. In one hand he had an old carpetbag and in the other he held a leather strap that was wrapped around several large, old volumes of books. I wondered if his photophobia was caused by eyestrain from excessive reading.

"I am Phineas Jones, dealer in rare books," the man said as he approached the front desk. "I was wondering if I could obtain lodgings for a few days."

"Of course, sir," the clerk said as he turned the registration ledger towards the man. "Allow me to get a bellman to carry your valise and books for you, sir."

"Carrying my bag would be most welcome," the man said in a creaky voice as he put the carpetbag down to sign the registry. "However, I would prefer carrying my books myself. They represent some valuable merchandise and I would be remiss if I didn't care for them."

"Yes sir," the clerk said, signaling for a bellman.

Mr. Jones's reluctance to allow someone else to carry his books caught my attention. After all, if the books were extremely valuable I would expect them to be packed into a trunk or bag, not carried from a leather strap. I looked at the books and saw that several had pages that were not trimmed neatly. This could be a sign of age for the books or it could mean that, although the covers of the books were old, perhaps the contents of the books were not. The battleship plans had been described to me as a large rolled bundle of paper, as long as a walking stick and with the diameter of a platter. I wondered if the sheets of plans could be cut into rectangles and bound in a book. Reassembling the plans would be like fitting together the various mother-of-pearl pieces that make up the design on a lacquer box, but the ability to disguise the roll of plans as common books might make the effort worth it.

There was a pause in the activity in the lobby so I thought this might be a good opportunity to write another note to Sigerson-san and apprise him of the two new guests at the Mampei. However, before I could take pen in hand, there was a commotion at the door of the hotel and another guest walked in. This man was in a brown suit and a neat bowler hat. His face had bushy half-whiskers in the style gaijin call mutton-chops. He wore gold-rimmed glasses and had a pleasant smile on his face.

"Can I help you, sir?" the desk clerk asked.

"Yes, you can. I am Professor Nicholas Baltimore, the musicologist," the man said with an American accent. "I would like a room for a few days as I investigate the indigenous musical instruments for this area of Japan. In addition to my luggage, I have a collection of Japanese musical instruments and I would like them stored in my room."

"Certainly, sir," the clerk responded.

I wasn't totally sure what a "musicologist" was, but the answer became clearer as Professor Baltimore's luggage was brought into the hotel. One bellman had a large bundle of *fue*. The flutes were made from hardwood and bamboo and represented the types of fue seen in various parts of Japan. There was an assortment of small *taiko* and *okedo* drums, including a beautiful okedo with black lacquer sides and white silk ropes connecting the drumheads on each side of the okedo, pulling the drumheads tight. The professor also had two *shamisen* string instruments, their distinctive shape clearly visible in the carrying bags that contained them. There were no koto,

I suppose because our Japanese zither can sometimes be quite long, but otherwise it was an impressive collection of instruments that the Professor had gathered during his time in Japan.

I finished my note to Sigerson-san and had a hotel messenger run it to Col. Ashworth's house because the Colonel had not returned to the bar. Within an hour the Colonel made an appearance at the hotel. He came over to greet me, shaking my hand and leaving a note deposited in it as he did so. Then he retreated to his station in the hotel bar.

When I had a chance to do it surreptitiously, I opened the note and read it.

My dear Doctor:

Thank you for the update. Whoever has the plans will not want to stop the auction—their greed will win out over their sense of caution—so the people gathering at the Mampei are there for the auction. Observe carefully and try to keep a close watch on the Major's room. Do not do anything to alert the Major that you know about the plans.

Sigerson

I settled into my comfortable chair in the lobby and proceeded to observe the front desk closely. As I sat there I thought it would be a good idea to stay at the Mampei, at least for a few days. Since I had already established a reason for being at the Mampei (the fictitious work being done on my house), I thought it would be easy to say the work involved more disruption than I anticipated and that I would like to take a room.

I registered at the hotel and got my room key. Then I quickly dashed off two notes. One was to inform Sigerson-san of my plans to stay at the hotel and the other was to Hosokawa-san to send me a bag with clothes suitable for a few days. I gave the note to Hosokawa-san to the hotel, asking them to have the messenger wait for the bag and put the bag in my room. Then I wandered into the bar to deliver my note for Sigerson-san to Col. Ashworth, once more using foolishly clandestine methods.

After that chore I decided it was a good time to check on my patient and I went to Major Staudinger's room. There I found the Major better, thanks to the liquids and rest. I was checking his temperature when there was a firm knock at the door.

I went to the door and opened it. There was the formidable Miss Trees. I don't know who was more surprised when I opened the door, Miss Trees or myself.

"You're not Major Staudinger," she said rudely, looking at my Japanese face.

"No I'm not. I am Doctor Watanabe and Major Staudinger is a patient of mine. He is feeling a bit under the weather."

Surprise was replaced by astonishment. "Your English is bloody good!" she said. "After spending ten months in this country I don't expect any Japanese to have English as good as yours."

I wasn't sure if I should be insulted or flattered by her blunt assessment of my language skills. "May I ask what you want to see Major Staudinger about?" I said. "He is still rather weak from his illness."

"From his name I guessed that Major Staudinger is Swabian. I spent three years roaming around Swabia examining the natural history of the district. I speak Schwaebisch, the local dialect. I stopped by because I would like to hear that language again," she said.

Normally I would have turned her away when I had a sick patient but Major Staudinger looked much improved and I did not think it would harm his health to talk to Miss

Trees. More importantly, I was interested in observing how the two interacted. "You can talk to him for a few minutes but please do not tire him out," I said.

Miss Trees glared at me. Evidently she was the one used to giving orders, not having orders given to her. But I can glare too, if it's required to protect a patient's health, and I gave her a look as stern as the one she was giving me.

She averted her eyes first. "All right," she said grudgingly.

Miss Trees entered the room and said something in German to the Major. The Major looked surprised and replied. I had acquired a rough reading knowledge of German so I could scan Western medical and scientific journals, which are often published in German. However, reading a language and speaking a language are two very different things, especially if the language is being spoken in a dialect. From the tone of her voice and her brusqueness it did not sound like Miss Trees was exchanging pleasantries but perhaps her demeanor in German was as rough as her demeanor in English.

After they talked for a few minutes it appeared as if the Major was starting to tire so I stepped in and asked them to end their conversation. For once Miss Trees obeyed my instructions without resistance and she said goodbye to the Major and left.

Major Staudinger looked at me and said, "That was a surprise. I have not heard someone speak Schwaebisch since I came to Japan."

I searched the Major's face to see if I could tell if he was being genuine to me or if he was covering up the content of his conversation with Miss Trees. I could not tell which was true by simply looking at him.

"Do you think I will be well enough to go to the dining room for supper?" he asked.

"You are improving but I would prefer you to rest another day. The hotel is happy to bring meals to your room so I wouldn't exert myself."

"I understand you, Doctor, but I would still like to make the effort if I can."

"Of course Major, you will do no permanent damage if you decide to push things a little bit and want to go to the dining room this evening. However, please do not take an extended time eating and return to your room as soon as possible so you can continue resting." I wondered if the Major's interest in leaving his sick bed and going to the dining room was prompted by his conversation with Miss Trees or if it was motivated by something else.

Deciding I might be able to discover more about the Major's motivation if I observed him at supper I took my leave and left his room.

As soon as I entered the hall I saw a fleeting wisp of white at the end of the hall where the corridor turned to go down another hallway. At first I confusedly thought I had seen a wisp of white smoke but then I suddenly realized that the brief flash of white I had seen was not smoke at all. It was white hair, the kind of white hair I had seen on Mr. Jones. Was he standing at the corner of the corridor watching the door of Major Staudinger? Was he waiting for a chance to enter the Major's room to talk to him?

I sprinted to the end of the corridor but when I was able to see around the corner I was confronted by an empty hallway. Did my eyes deceive me?

Irritated, I spun around quickly. As I did so I was able to see a face disappearing from the other corner of the corridor. Once again I ran down the hallway and as I turned the corner I almost ran directly into Kurihara-san. The Assistant Manager looked as startled as I was.

"Is something wrong, Doctor?" he asked.

"Did you pass anyone when you came here?"

"No, I didn't. I was just coming to check on Major Staudinger."

"He seems to be much improved. In fact, he was even talking about going to the dining room for supper."

"That's very good news," Kurihara-san said. "Thank you for your help in this matter."

"It's nothing," I answered.

Kurihara-san gave a respectful bow and he turned to return to the lobby area. I stood looking at his retreating back. The face I saw was too fleeting to make identification possible, but the face did have black hair and looked Japanese. What possible reason could Kurihara-san have for observing the corridor in front of Major Staudinger's room? Was he stalking the door like the elusive white-haired watcher at the other end of the hall?

When I was in England I saw a stage play about an ocean liner. The English called it a farce. The plot revolved around a series of romantic misunderstandings and it had a large cast of people popping into and out of staterooms. The set was a corridor in the liner and people were always running from one end of the ship's hallway to the other, running away from or pursuing other characters in the play.

The English found this uproariously funny. In my current situation, where I had been running from one end of a hallway to the other, I didn't find it funny. In fact, I felt like a complete *baka*. Of course, acting like a fool is not the same as being a fool but I was discouraged by my lack of talent in discovering who was observing Major Staudinger's room. I was sure Sigerson-san would know. Dejected, I went to my room and prepared myself to go to supper.

The main dining room at the Mampei serves

Western style food. Gaijin are often surprised at how good Western food can be in Japan but they don't understand our Japanese obsession with doing things properly. For instance, when I was taught *zazen*, Zen meditation, the priest who instructed me said there was only one way to do things properly for everything. It was my job to learn this one way.

After studying in Europe and seeing the bewildering variety in human behavior I no longer believe there is only one proper way to do all things. However, the desire to do things properly has been ingrained in my nature and perhaps in the nature of most Japanese. This applies to being a Western chef as well as being a Dutch Medicine physician.

When I arrived at the dining room it was already quite full. Most of the tables were occupied by hotel guests engaged in various stages of dining. Most notably, I saw Miss Trees sitting alone at a table attacking a large bowl of soup with obvious relish. Count Kirovsky was at a table flanked by a silver bucket with iced champagne. There was a small Western orchestra in a corner of the room and Professor Baltimore was sitting near the orchestra listening to the music with obvious enjoyment. Sitting in a corner, concentrating on an open book next to his dinner plate, Mr. Jones seemed oblivious to his surroundings.

I had just started to peruse the menu when Major Staudinger entered. He was dressed in his military uniform and looked pale. I started to rise to see if I could assist him. He saw me, smiled, and raised a hand to indicate that he didn't need assistance, although he certainly looked like he did.

From nowhere Kurihara-san appeared to guide the Major to a table. Even though I had not spotted him, Kurihara-san was obviously watching the occupants of the dining room and his interest in the Major confirmed my feeling that he might have been watching the Major's room earlier.

Most of the dishes on the menu were chicken-based, which made sense because chicken was easily available in Karuizawa and fish, lamb, pork, and beef were not. I ordered and as I started eating the first course the orchestra began playing a light and soothing selection. Halfway through the musical selection I saw Count Kirovsky hand the waiter a piece of paper. The waiter took the paper to the orchestra leader, who looked at it and bowed slightly to the Count. When the orchestra finished its piece it started on a lively tune that I assumed to be Russian. Interestingly enough, as this piece played Major Staudinger also called a waiter over and handed him a note to give to the orchestra leader.

After the Russian piece finished the orchestra started on a selection that I assumed was German. There seemed to be an element of national pride in the beginning battle over the dinner music because Count Kirovsky looked quite annoyed by Major Staudinger, and he sent another note to the orchestra. After the orchestra began playing the Count's piece, Major Staudinger responded in turn. As the orchestra began playing the Major's request, the Count, now positively glowering at Major Staudinger, sent another note to the orchestra.

The orchestra seemed tired but they couldn't stop playing while patrons were sending them requests. The Major sat for several minutes, as if weighing whether he wanted to keep this silly competition with Count Kirovsky going. He seemed to make a decision and wrote no more notes to the orchestra, instead focusing his attention on his entrée.

When the orchestra finished Count Kirovsky's final request they seemed relieved as they left the dining room for a well-deserved intermission. Major Staudinger finished his meal first, since he had a light supper suitable for a man recovering from an illness, and left. In a few minutes

Professor Baltimore and Miss Trees did the same. As I finished my meal and left the dining room I noticed that Mr. Jones was still immersed in his book.

As I returned to my room I was frustrated. I had observed Sigerson-san on several occasions and I thought I had learned some of his techniques. As with my first meeting with him, however, I learned that his observations and deductions, while simple and even obvious once they were explained, were neither simple nor obvious if another person had to make them on his own. I had no idea what was happening and my only plan was to write a long letter to Sigerson-san describing what had occurred, hoping he would be able to draw the necessary conclusions.

As I proceeded down the corridor I detected someone following me. I turned and saw the book dealer, Mr. Jones, behind me. Dressed in black and hunched over like a menacing spider, his appearance gave me a definite feeling of unease. Perhaps because of my frustration at not being able to apply Sigerson-san's methods, I decided to confront Mr. Jones directly.

I turned and said to him, "Hello, my name is Doctor Junichi Watanabe."

"And I am Phineas Jones," he said.

"If I may be so bold as to ask, is your room in this direction?"

"No it is not. I am actually following you."

The brazenness of his confession shocked me. "May I ask why?"

Mr. Jones started unfolding himself and straightening his posture until I was standing there in astonishment, looking up at him. He seemed to grow in front of my very eyes. He then took the colored glasses from his nose and pulled off a white wig from his head. He gave me a familiar, fleeting smile.

"Sigerson-san!" I exclaimed.

"Quite. I was following you for the same reason I watched you when you were in Major Staudinger's room. I was afraid that the desperate characters we are dealing with might try to harm you if they found out you were trying to thwart their efforts to sell the battleship plans."

I had no response to this. I just stood gawking at Sigerson-san, stupefied and amazed that the ancient book dealer had transformed into my house guest.

"Observing you in Major Staudinger's room did have an unexpected benefit, however," Sigerson-san continued. "While there I was able to observe that the Assistant Manager of this hotel, Kurihara, was also watching the Major's room." Sigerson-san raised his voice, "In fact, unless I am badly mistaken, Kurihara is observing both of us at this moment. Isn't that correct, Mr. Kurihara?"

From the end of the corridor, Kurihara-san stepped into the light. "Yes, it is." He walked to us. "You'll forgive me, I hope, because I was curious why someone would want to check into this hotel while disguised. I was actually keeping an eye on you, not the Doctor."

Sigerson-san looked a little crestfallen. His disguise fooled me completely but somehow Kurihara-san was able to penetrate it. "How did you know I was in disguise?" he asked.

"Your hands. They are not the hands of an old man."

"Ah! Very observant. That was foolish of me not to think of that. Next time I must wear gloves or apply makeup to my hands. But I think you are also sailing under false colors, so to speak. You claim to be the Assistant Manager for this hotel but apparently you have recently appeared here. In hotels the management is almost exclusively composed of people who have come up through the ranks at that hotel. Therefore, although you obviously have great authority here, I believe you are not truly a manager at this establishment."

I had noticed the hands of Mr. Jones and had not made the same conclusion as Kurihara-san. Just as importantly, what Sigerson-san was saying about the management at a top hotel was true and the sudden appearance of Kurihara-san in the position of Assistant Manager at the Mampei had not aroused my suspicions, either. I felt I had learned nothing from my contact with Sigerson-san except that I was unable to apply his methods.

Kurihara-san gave a smile. "I will happily discuss who I am if you will tell me why you are here at the Mampei."

Sigerson-san stared at Kurihara-san for a brief moment, as if assessing the man. Then he said, "Actually I am working with Minister Fraser to recover the battleship plans so recently stolen. We have enlisted the aid of Dr. Watanabe in this effort, although his motivation is a patriotic one because he knows it will help Japan to have us recover the plans."

Kurihara-san seemed surprised that Sigerson-san was so forthright and he said, "Since you have, as they say, laid your cards on the table, then I will do the same." He took a card from his pocket and held it out for us to see. "You won't be able to read this, but perhaps the Doctor can tell you what it is."

I had never seen anything like it before, although I recognized what it was. At the top of the card was the Imperial seal of the 16-petal chrysanthemum, plus kanji that informed me that the card identified Shozo Kurihara-san of the Security Branch of the Imperial Foreign Ministry. I didn't even know there was a Security Branch at the Foreign Ministry, but I informed Sigerson-san what the identification card said.

"So we have the same objective," Sigerson-san said. "We both want to retrieve the battleship plans and return them to the Japanese government."

"Precisely," Kurihara-san said.

"Then we don't have much time," Sigerson-san said. "Were you able to follow what just happened in the dining room?"

"I think so," Kurihara-san said, "but I'd like your opinion."

Kurihara-san's statement made me feel very stupid, indeed, because I didn't know what was going on, although apparently he and Sigerson-san shared that knowledge.

"The musical contest between Major Staudinger and Count Kirovsky was obviously an auction." Sigerson-san said. "Each time they had the orchestra play a piece it raised the bid by some set amount that had been agreed to beforehand."

"That is what I thought," Kurihara-san said.

"But who was holding the auction?" I asked.

"The form of the auction should give you the clue to that," Sigerson-san said.

"The American music professor! Professor Baltimore!" I exclaimed.

"Exactly. Do you know his room number?" Sigerson asked.

"Of course," Kurihara-san said. "Please follow me."

We rushed through the halls of the Mampei until we

came to a room. Kurihara-san knocked on the door and waited. After a few minutes he took a set of keys from his pocket and put one in the lock. He unlocked Professor Baltimore's room and we entered.

Along one wall were the musical instruments but otherwise the room looked empty. "The wardrobe!" I exclaimed, and went over to the cabinet and opened it. It was empty.

"The Professor has flown," Sigerson-san said.

"I have men I can send both up and down the Nakasendo road. We'll intercept him."

Sigerson-san shook his head. "I'm sure this gang has planned an escape more subtle than taking the main road out of Karuizawa. It might be difficult to find him. Besides, the battleship plans have undoubtedly been transferred to the winner of the auction."

"But we can't let him get away," I said.

"I'm afraid he has already gotten away," Sigerson-san said. "But I have no doubt that, if I stay in this country, I will encounter Professor Baltimore again. I believe the Professor is probably like another Professor I knew, the late leader of the largest international crime syndicate extant, the same syndicate that I am sure Professor Baltimore is part of. By that I mean that both evil and criminal mischief done by this syndicate are unending and inexhaustible. I am sure that Professor Baltimore will once again be involved in crime here in Japan. However, our objective now is to recover the battleship plans and the reason the Professor has flown is that his business here was done."

Kurihara-san looked grim. "Then let us visit Count Kirovsky," he said.

Once again we went to another part of the Mampei and Kurihara-san knocked on the door. This time we got an answer. Count Kirovsky opened the door slightly and looked at us in surprise.

"What is it?" he demanded.

"I'm afraid we would like to enter your room, Count," Kurihara-san said.

"It is not convenient at this time," he said, starting to close the door.

Sigerson-san wedged his body in the door so it could not be shut. "I'm afraid this is not a matter of convenience, but of urgency," he said. He forced the door open and we all entered the Count's room.

"What is this outrage!" the Count shouted.

I saw the okedo drum in the corner of the room and pointed to it. It was the same black lacquer okedo that Professor Baltimore had. The drum, with the two drum heads held by criss-crossed white cords, would be a perfect hiding place for the plans. With the Count blustering protests, Sigerson-san went to the drum and struck it. Instead of a deep boom there was a muffled thump. There was definitely something inside the drum.

"Get out of my room!" the Count shouted. "And don't touch my possessions. That drum belongs to me. I purchased it from Professor Baltimore."

"That drum can't be sold," Kurihara-san said. "It is a valuable drum and one precious to His Imperial Majesty's government." He showed his identity card. "I am a member of the Security Branch of the Imperial Foreign Ministry and I am authorized to seize anything necessary to protect His Majesty's government."

"I am a member of the Russian Legation," Kirovsky thundered. "Taking one of my possessions is a breach of diplomatic protocol and will require the most severe retaliation from the Czar's government. You are playing with the possibility of war!"

This seemed to give both Kurihara-san and Sigerson-san some pause, but I had a sudden inspiration. "But you are traveling incognito, Count. You said so yourself when you checked in. Therefore you are not protected by diplomatic conventions. That drum has stolen material in it and we must recover it. After we recover it you can naturally have the drum back."

The Count's face turned red with anger. "What use do I have for that drum..."

Kurihara-san smiled. "The Doctor is quite right. You are traveling incognito so there is no need to observe the diplomatic necessities. Of course, Count, I'm sure you were not aware that stolen material was secreted inside that drum or you would never have accepted it so there is no need to involve you in the crime, either."

Sigerson-san had already seized the drum.

"But, but..." the Count spluttered. Before he could form his next thought we had all exited his room and slammed the door behind us.

In the hall we all looked at each other and burst out laughing. It was the first time I had seen Sigerson actually fully laugh, instead of giving a quick smile. Sigerson-san shook the drum and there was most definitely something inside it. In a few minutes we were in the Mampei's kitchen where we could obtain a knife to cut the cords holding the okedo together. The plans, neatly rolled and cushioned by cloth, were inside. Kurihara-san took possession of the plans with the promise that they would be safely delivered to the Imperial Navy Headquarters before the night was over.

"That was brilliant of you to remember the Count was traveling incognito," Sigerson-san said to me. "It was something I was completely unaware of. Once again, Doctor, you have proven invaluable."

I smiled. Even though I was not able to apply the deductive skills I saw in Sigerson-san, perhaps I was not so useless after all.

The Case of Hear No Evil

Sadly, we see so

much true evil in the world.

Must we hear it too?

"It's a very sad situation, I'm afraid; sad and totally inexplicable." Reverend Murchison picked up his teacup and blew across the top of the cup to cool down the liquid.

I could never understand why the English went to the trouble of boiling tea water and then spent equal time cooling it down. Talk of murder, however, caused Sigerson-san to forget about drinking his tea entirely. He put down his cup and leaned forward, concentration painted across his face.

"Can you tell us in detail what you know of the death?" Sigerson-san asked.

The Reverend Murchison looked surprised. He had stopped by my house to visit my Norwegian guest, Sigerson-san. The Reverend said he was just inquiring to see if Sigerson-san had any spiritual needs that needed tending to. Sigerson-san, who exhibited little spirituality of any kind, did not need tending to but when he heard that Reverend Murchison had details about the recent murder at the lodge of Reverend Robert Pearson, Sigerson-san suddenly had a desire to spend time with the gaijin holy man.

Reverend Murchison finished puffing on his tea, sipped it, and settled back in his chair with the satisfied air of a man who has an audience.

"I suppose I should give you a little background before I describe the terrible events of Tuesday last," he began. "Reverend Robert Pearson was from an independent Protestant denomination in Eastern Canada. He came to Japan almost ten years ago and he felt his first order of business was to learn the Japanese language. Of course, not every missionary in Japan feels this is really required. I, for instance, have been in Japan for almost four years but can speak almost no Japanese," Reverend Murchison revealed with some considerable pride.

"I rely on translators and local converts when doing missionary work, as do most of us here in Japan. Reverend Pearson, however, acquired the idea that spreading the gospel would be more effective if the missionary could speak directly to the people in their own language. To facilitate this he set up a Japanese language school as part of his church in Yokohama, but about a year ago he succumbed to the lure of this beautiful mountain retreat of Karuizawa and his denomination, at his urging, bought a lodge here where he could concentrate on operating his language school for missionaries. Are you familiar with the Cloud Lodge?"

Sigerson-san and I said we were not.

"Well, understanding something of the geography and layout of the Cloud Lodge is necessary for a full understanding of what transpired. The Cloud Lodge is so named because it is perched high on a cliff. From the back of the Lodge there is a magnificent view of the valley below, just as if you were sitting on a cloud. The Lodge has two stories. The lower story has the common rooms, now used as language classrooms, and cooking facilities. Upstairs the Lodge has several bedrooms and a study. The study is a bit unusual because it opens on to a small veranda where one can sit and look down at the valley. Since the cliff is steep and rocky, it is virtually impossible for a man to climb up to the veranda from the ground below. That is something that must be kept in mind.

"Last Tuesday Reverend Pearson had three language students with him at the Lodge: Mr. Lock, Mr. MacKenzie and Mr. Short. The students had been there several weeks studying Japanese but apparently there was a great deal of tension between Mr. Clarence Lock and Reverend Pearson. It seems it started over a minor theological argument over the concept of transubstantiation…"

"Excuse me," I said. "What is that?" This was an English word I had never heard.

"Ah, transubstantiation. It is the idea that the bread and wine used in Holy Communion will, in substance, change to the actual flesh and blood of Christ. The Roman Catholic Church and some other churches believe this but most Protestant churches do not adhere to the doctrine. In the sixteenth century the Council of Trent made an interesting comment about transubstantiation where it said…"

"Reverend?" Sigerson-san interrupted.

Reverend Murchison seemed surprised. "Yes?" He was not used to being interrupted.

"This discussion of the ecclesiastical aspects of transubstantiation is extremely interesting, I'm sure, but it would be helpful if we focused on the events of last Tuesday at the Cloud Lodge."

"Oh. Yes. Quite."

I was glad Sigerson-san stopped the Reverend. I know many gaijin are repelled at some of the foods we eat here in Japan. And as a doctor I am trained to keep a professional attitude about some of the more bestial aspects of the human body and human behavior. But the thought of actually consuming human flesh and blood in a religious act of ritual cannibalism was horrifying me, even if it was symbolic (which I was not completely sure it was, according to what the Reverend said).

The Reverend Murchison cleared his throat and continued.

"Well. In any case, this initial theological argument continued to fester between the two men. Frankly, Reverend Pearson could be quite prickly and was getting worse as he aged. I think that was one reason he was encouraged to give up his church in Yokohama to devote his attentions to teaching Japanese here in Karuizawa. Also, Mr. Lock has the righteous indignation and anger of youth, so it was an uncomfortable combination at Cloud Lodge. Since Mr. Lock was at Cloud Lodge to learn the Japanese language from Reverend Pearson, they were all forced to endure an unpleasant situation." Reverend Murchison looked at us archly. "Of course, things apparently just got worse between them as the days passed."

He took another sip of tea.

"Things came to a head between the two last Monday. I'm afraid I had an inadvertent role in precipitating that crisis and I witnessed a good part of it. I mentioned that Reverend Pearson was in Yokohama before he moved to Karuizawa. While in Yokohama he helped a Japanese woman find her way to Christ, something she was always grateful for. My current church is in Yokohama and I was summoned to this woman's bedside approximately a week ago. She was dying.

"My denomination is not the same as Reverend Pearson's but I've noticed that even Japanese Christians can't seem to understand the differences between different religious denominations, especially if they are both Protestant. Often it seems too much to ask of them to even differentiate between the Roman Church and Protestants," he said with a sniff of disdain. He saw the expression on my face and said, "I hope I've given no offense with my comments on the ability of Japanese to discern differences in Christian beliefs."

"Of course not, Reverend. We Japanese are usually very ecumenical in our religious beliefs and practices, which makes making fine ecclesiastical distinctions difficult. Besides, I've noticed that most gaijin can't explain the differences between Buddhist sects, such as Soto Zen, Nichiren, or Hongwanji. As with your complaints about differentiating between Protestants and Catholics, some gaijin don't even understand the difference between Buddhism and Shinto."

Reverend Murchison blinked at me, not sure if he had been agreed with or insulted. Sigerson-san shot me a hard look, annoyed that I had distracted the Reverend from his story. I smiled at the Reverend and took a sip of tea, which seemed to encourage him to continue.

"Yes. Well. In any case, the woman called me to her bedside and gave me something to give to Reverend Pearson. It was a small case. I opened it and inside was a pearl—a quite beautiful pearl that was attached to a gold chain. I am no judge of pearls but this one was quite large and lustrous, with a deep pink color. It was obviously very valuable. The woman said the pearl was a gift to Reverend Pearson for educating her about Christianity and she asked me if I would make sure he received it. I so promised and, I was told, the next day she passed on.

"I was naturally quite nervous about having such a valuable keepsake in my possession. My denomination keeps a small cabin as a retreat here in Karuizawa and I decided to visit it. So, after performing my Sunday duties, on Monday morning I boarded the train from Tokyo and came here.

"Before I visited my cabin I decided to go to Cloud Lodge and pass on the pearl to Reverend Pearson. I was determined to relieve myself of the burden of something so valuable. When I got to the Lodge I found Reverend Pearson in the main room with Mr. Lock, Mr. MacKenzie, and Mr. Short. The Reverend was in the midst of giving them a Japanese lesson. When he saw me, Reverend Pearson welcomed me and asked me why I was making an unexpected visit. I said I had something to give him and that perhaps it would be better to speak in private. I added that it was good news. To this day I rue making that addition because I feel that conducting our business in public was the root cause of the subsequent tragedy.

"If it's good news, Reverend Pearson said, then please feel free to announce it in public. He said they could all use good news.

"I told him his former parishioner was dead. He responded by saying that surely wasn't the good news. I told him of course not, although the good lady had lived a full life and went to her Maker in the bosom of Christ. What was good news was that she had left him a legacy to show how much she appreciated his bringing her to Christianity. Then I did another foolish thing. I withdrew the case from my pocket and opened it. The four men crowded around me and there was an audible gasp from them as they saw the pearl nestled in the case." Reverend Murchison hung his head. "I freely admit that was a mistake. I am truly sorry that I didn't insist that Reverend Pearson and I conduct our business in private but I had no idea of the bad blood that already existed between Mr. Lock and Reverend Pearson or what a fight this would cause."

"What happened?" Sigerson-san asked.

"Reverend Pearson was naturally pleased at receiving such a magnificent gift, although he was naturally sad at the passing of his former parishioner. He started talking about how the pearl would secure his retirement when he returned to Canada. Mr. Lock expressed surprise at Reverend Pearson's statements and said that surely the pearl should be turned over to the church. Mr. Lock pointed out that the proceeds from the pearl could fund missionary work in Japan for several years. Reverend Pearson said this was none of Mr. Lock's business and that the pearl had been bequeathed to him personally. Mr. Lock said none of them came to Japan for personal gain, but to spread the truth of Christianity and that the pearl was rightfully the property of the church."

"And whose property was it?" Sigerson-san asked.

Reverend Murchison shifted uncomfortably in his seat. "Well. Yes. That is an interesting question. It is not clear. Normally a gift is considered the personal property of the recipient, but in this case, with such an expensive gift… well, I suppose the issue could be debated on either side."

"Please continue," Sigerson-san said.

"Well, there is not much more I can say from my own knowledge. Reverend Pearson and Mr. Lock engaged in a heated argument and it ended with Mr. Lock leaving Cloud Lodge in a fit of anger. Reverend Pearson excused himself and retired up the stairs to the study on the second floor. That's when Mr. MacKenzie and Mr. Short explained to me the previous argument over transubstantiation and the tension they were all living under because of it. The next day Reverend Pearson was dead and Mr. Lock is accused of killing him."

"How exactly did he die?" Sigerson asked.

"The authorities believe that Reverend Pearson and Mr. Lock got into an argument about the pearl on the veranda of Cloud Lodge. Somehow during the argument Reverend Pearson was pushed or fell from the veranda to his death. In any case, the pearl is missing and Mr. Lock claims no knowledge about where the pearl is. The local authorities do not believe Mr. Lock and have placed him in jail, pending the arrival of the proper authorities from

Tokyo to decide what should be done about the situation. As I said, it is sad and inexplicable."

It was obvious that the Reverend had no more facts to provide, although he seemed ready to provide extraneous speculation and silly theories. As soon as it was politely possible, Sigerson-san assured Reverend Murchison that his spiritual needs were not lacking and got the Reverend out of my house.

As the door closed on the departing Reverend, Sigerson-san looked at me and said, "What do you think of the story of the missing pearl and the death of Reverend Pearson?"

"I think you are intrigued by both and wish to become involved in this investigation."

Sigerson-san gave a short, almost barking laugh. "You know me too well, Doctor."

I shrugged. "It's easy to observe when a bird wants to fly."

Sigerson-san gave another short laugh. "Will you help me?"

"Of course. I've found that I like flying, too."

"Good. Let's go to the Karuizawa city jail and talk to Mr. Lock."

With Sigerson-san, who was as impatient as a child when it came to pursuing his strange hobby of crime solving, sometimes the motto of "no sooner said than done" applied so in a few minutes we were walking into Karuizawa.

I confess I had never been to the Karuizawa jail so I had to ask where it was located. It was a nondescript, small building near the center of town. Although the building was impeccably clean it somehow still managed to have a dingy and depressing feeling to it. Perhaps this was because I knew what its function was, not because of anything external to the structure. We Japanese are good at projecting our feelings onto nature so I suppose we do the same thing with innocent buildings.

We asked to see Mr. Lock and were immediately taken to the back of the building. There were two cells. The bars for the cells were made from a lattice of wood reinforced at the joints by straps of iron. One of the cells was empty and the other held a gaijin in his mid-twenties; Mr. Lock. Mr. Lock had dark hair and a rather pinched expression to his face. He was intently reading a small book which, upon closer examination, I realized was a western Bible. When he saw us he closed the Bible and quickly leapt to his feet. Here was apparently a man of strong religious convictions but he also appeared to be a man who took hasty action. I wondered if that combination had led to the death of Reverend Pearson.

"Are you from the Canadian Legation?" he said to Sigerson-san. "Are you here to get me out? I am innocent. Can you help me?"

"We are not from the Legation or any government agency," Sigerson-san said. "However, if you are truly innocent we may be able to help you. That depends on you and your willingness to answer our questions honestly and accurately."

"Who are you, sir?"

"My name is Sigerson. I have had some experience in criminal investigation in Europe. I am willing to look into the case of Reverend Pearson to see if I can discern anything that would help discover your involvement or lack of involvement in his death. This is my colleague, Dr. Watanabe. He has helped me with investigations here in Japan."

Mr. Lock looked at me and gave a bow. "*Hajimemashite. Watashi wa Lock Clarence desu,*" he said in passable Japanese. This was the work of Reverend Pearson, I thought.

"Are you willing to answer some questions for us?" Sigerson-san asked.

"Anything! This whole incident has been a nightmare but I can assure you I had nothing to do with the death of Reverend Pearson."

"Yet you argued with him. I understand that sometimes those arguments were quite heated."

Mr. Lock hung his head. "I know. The foundation of our antagonism was my religious arrogance. I realize that now. Transubstantiation was a theological matter that our church doctrine really takes no official position on and therefore I had no right to press my arguments so forcefully. I should not have gotten upset when Reverend Pearson did not adopt my point of view."

"I am not talking about your argument on theology. I'm talking about your view regarding the pearl that was given to Reverend Pearson."

Mr. Lock sighed. "I thought of all the good the pearl could do in financing our church's future activities in Japan and I may have spoken out of turn. It seemed that Reverend Pearson was focused on what the pearl could do for him, assuring him a comfortable retirement. I realize now I was too harsh and too strident in my comments to Reverend Pearson. I should have gently persuaded the Reverend to consider donating the pearl to the church instead of insisting that the pearl was the property of the church. But that doesn't mean that I was willing to kill the Reverend over the pearl."

"Do you know where the pearl is?"

"I swear I do not. I don't know what happened to the pearl or why it's missing. The pearl was already missing when I came upon the scene. I know the Reverend was already dead."

"Please tell me exactly what happened on the day the Reverend died," Sigerson-san asked.

"On Tuesday morning my fellow students and I decided to take a walk. I admit I was still upset about the argument the day before. My two companions discussed it with me, pointing out that as brothers in Christ it was unseemly for me to argue with Reverend Pearson, especially in front of Reverend Murchison, who is from another denomination. They also pointed out that our church has no official policy about how gifts from parishioners should be handled, no matter how magnificent."

Mr. Lock looked at us and said, "I'm afraid I have a fearsome temper and a tendency to go off half-cocked. It is something I pray about but the Lord, in His infinite wisdom, has for some reason not chosen to relieve me of the burden of my temper. However, I saw the wisdom of my fellow students' counsel and therefore I took leave of my companions and hurried back to Cloud Lodge. I swear that my intention was to apologize to Reverend Pearson, but I wanted to do it in private. I admit that I might have wanted to restate my views about what should be done with the pearl but I had no intention of getting into another argument with him.

"When I got to the Lodge I realized that Reverend Pearson was not on the main floor. He spent a great deal of time on the veranda outside the study reading so I started up the stairs. I was halfway up the stairs when I heard Reverend Pearson shouting. I think he said, 'Don't' or 'Go away.' I rushed up the stairs because I could tell from his tone he was very distressed and upset. Then I heard a piercing cry from the Reverend. By the time I got to the veranda it was empty. At first I was puzzled. I couldn't understand where the Reverend was or the person he was shouting at. Then, with a sick feeling in my stomach, I looked over the rail of the veranda and at the ground below. There I saw the body of the Reverend Pearson. He was smashed against the rocks at the bottom of the cliff that backs up to Cloud Lodge."

"Was there anybody else on the veranda?" Sigerson-san asked.

"No. I don't know who Reverend Pearson was shouting at but there was no one else on the veranda."

"Could they have slipped past you?" Sigerson-san said.

"It would be impossible. The door into the study can be seen from the top of the stairs. One cannot leave the study without being seen from the stairs. If you go to Cloud Lodge you can see that for yourself."

"An excellent idea," Sigerson-san said. With that Sigerson-san and I took our leave. A mournful Mr. Lock watched us go.

"What do you think about Mr. Lock's tale?" Sigerson-san asked me.

"It seems strange, to say the least."

"Do you believe him?"

"I don't know."

"I think he is telling the truth."

"Why?"

"Because it would be easy for him to say he arrived to find Reverend Pearson already dead. Instead he says he heard Reverend Pearson yelling at someone."

"But he also said that he didn't see anyone leave the study," I protested.

"Precisely. That is why I believe he is telling the truth. If he was going to say he heard Reverend Pearson still alive when he arrived he should also say he saw someone leaving the study. The fact that he doesn't makes me believe that Mr. Lock is telling us the truth, even though this truth makes for a very puzzling set of circumstances."

As usual I couldn't disagree with Sigerson-san's logic, although I privately thought that perhaps being too logical about human behavior could be a disadvantage. Sometimes even intelligent people tell lies that fail the test of consistency. In fact, the only consistent factor about humans is that we are often inconsistent.

Cloud Lodge was north of Karuizawa towards Usui Pass. The walk to the Lodge was pleasant even though it was all uphill. When we got to the Lodge we found a rustic two-story structure nestled amongst the trees. Behind the Lodge, however, the forest abruptly ended because the building was perched on the edge of a cliff.

We knocked and the door was opened by a sandy-haired man in his early twenties. He introduced himself as Mr. MacKenzie. When he found out we were visiting in an effort to help Mr. Lock he let us in immediately.

Inside we met another young man, Mr. Short. Mr. Short had a handsome face and dark hair. Both gentlemen seemed sincere and genuinely distressed by Reverend Pearson's death and the possible involvement of Mr. Lock.

"Can you tell us about last Tuesday?" Sigerson-san asked.

"Of course," Mr. MacKenzie answered. "Both Mr. Short and I had counseled Mr. Lock about his outburst over the pearl. Are you familiar with the pearl and the events that preceded it?"

We said we were.

"The three of us went for a walk. Mr. Short and I thought that this would be the ideal setting for a sincere talk about the conflict between Mr. Lock and Reverend Pearson. At first Mr. Lock was resistant to changing his position but through persuasion and an appeal to his Christian sense of tolerance we were able to change his opinion. He said he wanted to go to Reverend Pearson and ask for forgiveness and started back to the Lodge on his own."

"But you didn't completely believe you were successful in convincing Mr. Lock," Sigerson-san said.

"Why do you say that?" Mr. Short asked.

"Because you followed Mr. Lock back to the Lodge almost immediately, afraid that he and Reverend Pearson might get into another argument."

Both Mr. Short and Mr. MacKenzie looked at each other, with Mr. MacKenzie's face getting the red glow of a Japanese who had consumed too much alcohol. "Yes, you are right," Mr. MacKenzie said. "We were a bit worried that Mr. Lock wasn't completely convinced that he had gone too far in his protestations about the pearl and we decided to return to the Lodge a few minutes after Mr. Lock left us."

"And what did you find?"

"As we entered the Lodge we found Mr. Lock coming down the stairs. He was agitated and clearly in distress. He said the Reverend was at the base of the cliff and seemed lifeless. He was rushing to find a way down the cliff so he could render aid to Reverend Pearson."

"Did he say anything else?"

"Yes," Mr. Short said. "He said that when he came to the Lodge he thought he heard Reverend Pearson shouting at someone to leave but when he rushed up to the veranda it was empty. That's when he said he looked over the railing and saw Reverend Pearson."

"Did you or Mr. MacKenzie see anyone leaving the Lodge as you approached it?" Sigerson-san asked.

Mr. Short hung his head and said, "No. I'm afraid we didn't. I actually searched the Lodge as Mr. Lock and Mr. MacKenzie circled around to the bottom of the cliff to check on the condition of Reverend Pearson. It occurred to me that if someone else was at the Lodge they might be hiding."

"And the result of your search?"

Mr. Short's head sunk even lower on his chest. "I'm afraid there was no one. Only Mr. Lock and Reverend Pearson were at the Lodge when Reverend Pearson died."

Sigerson-san digested this for a moment, then said, "Can we examine the veranda?"

"Of course."

Mr. Short and Mr. MacKenzie led us upstairs and through a door near the top of the stairs. There was a small study with bookshelves and a desk. The small desk occupied one corner, facing the wall. There was a door on the opposite wall that led to the outside veranda.

The veranda area itself was rather small with a round table and two chairs. I walked over to the rail and looked over. It was a long drop to the rocky ground below and I could see why Reverend Pearson died after such a fall. Death must have been almost instantaneous.

I noted with interest that it would be very difficult—perhaps impossible—for a man to scale the cliff and the side of the Lodge to reach the veranda from the bottom of the cliff. If Reverend Pearson was talking to someone on the veranda just before he died then the only way for that person to leave the veranda was through the study and into the hall where Mr. Lock should have been able to see him. The study was too small to allow anyone to hide in it but even if someone managed to elude Mr. Lock, Mr. Short said that he searched the Lodge and found no one. Yet, if Mr. Lock had pushed Reverend Pearson over the railing of the veranda to his death, why did he insist he heard Reverend Pearson talking to someone?

"Is the veranda as it was the day Reverend Pearson died?" Sigerson-san said.

"Yes it is," Mr. MacKenzie said.

"Actually there are some small changes," Mr. Short said.

"What kind of changes?"

"On the day Reverend Pearson died there was a small bowl of fruit on that table. We've since removed it because we didn't want the fruit to go rotten. Also, on that table was the open box that contained the pearl," Mr. Short said.

"That's right," Mr. MacKenzie said. "I had forgotten that. Are such details important, Mr. Sigerson?"

"They can be. Right now there are pieces missing from this puzzle so it is impossible to evaluate what will prove important and what will merely be a distraction. Therefore, please tell me anything you can even if it seems unimportant."

"There was one other thing," Mr. Short said.

"What was it?"

"There were some pieces of fruit scattered on the ground."

"Did it look like there was a struggle?" Sigerson-san asked.

"No, it just looked like some fruit had fallen from the table. Perhaps Reverend Pearson knocked them out of the fruit bowl by accident."

Sigerson-san seemed to think about this for a few moments. Then he said, "Can I ask you to vacate the veranda for a few minutes while I make a close inspection of it?"

Both Mr. Short and Mr. MacKenzie seemed a bit surprised by this request, but Mr. MacKenzie said, "Of course, sir."

Having seen Sigerson-san at work on several occasions now I was not surprised that he would want to make a close inspection of the scene. Along with Mr. Short and Mr. MacKenzie, I went into the study. Sigerson-san immediately pulled a magnifying glass I had given him out of his pocket and he started a minute examination of every inch of the veranda. Mr. Short and Mr. MacKenzie seemed fascinated by Sigerson-san's detailed inspection of the table, railing, chairs, and even the floor of the veranda. After watching him for a few minutes myself, I started to divert my attention to the study to see if I could use Sigerson-san's methods to give me more information about what kind of man Reverend Pearson was.

On the desk was an open book. I glanced at the book and saw that it was written in Japanese. It was a travel guide about the various regions in the country. I had been told Reverend Pearson knew enough Japanese to teach it but his ability to read Japanese was still quite impressive. Many gaijin can speak Japanese but not read it.

The rest of the study was quite neat with all the rest of the books neatly shelved and gathered together by topic. There were a few knickknacks on the desk. Perhaps they were things Reverend Pearson had gathered during his travels in Japan. One especially caught my eye. It was a small carved statue of three monkeys. Each monkey was slightly larger than a *netsuke* and they were all sitting down. The first monkey had its hands over its eyes. The second monkey had its hands over its mouth. The third monkey had its hands over its ears.

As I stared at the little statue I became very excited because I thought of Reverend Pearson's last words. Mr. Lock said he thought they were 'Don't' or 'Go away,' but he was not sure. Mr. Lock's confusion over these words raised an interesting possibility that required more information. The need for this information was not a guess but a logical deduction drawn from Mr. Lock's uncertainty. I wondered if this was how Sigerson-san's incredible mind worked and I received a jolt of excitement at this possible glimpse into his thought process.

I had to contain my excitement as Sigerson-san finished his inspection of the veranda and then asked to inspect the study. We moved into the hall and I waited for the completion of Sigerson-san's examination of the study with growing impatience. I knew his physical examination of the scene was important but I was anxious to confirm something that might provide Sigerson-san more information.

When Sigerson-san was done with his inspection we thanked Mr. Short and Mr. MacKenzie and we started back to town.

Sigerson-san was characteristically lost in thought.

"Sigerson-san?"

"Yes, Doctor?"

"I would like to return to the jail."

"Whatever for?"

"I have a question that I want to ask Mr. Lock, one we should have asked before."

"Oh? What is it?"

I became nervous. Sigerson-san's methodology depended on pure deduction and I had a sudden insight looking at a small statue. "Can I tell you after Mr. Lock answers my question? I'm afraid I will be very embarrassed if he doesn't answer the way I hope he will."

Sigerson-san gave me that penetrating look of his. Then he said, "Of course, Doctor. I think I understand some of what happened on that veranda, but I am still baffled about what Mr. Lock heard."

"What happened?"

"Reverend Pearson was sitting at his desk in the study and he stood up suddenly. You can tell that from scrapes in the rug where Reverend Pearson's chair was violently shoved back. The Reverend ran to the veranda. There the picture is less clear. There are fresh scratches on the railing of the veranda but they are small scratches so they weren't made when Reverend Pearson went over the rail of the veranda. I think I know what they may be but I am not completely sure."

"My question may lend light to that issue."

I said no more. I had learned a great deal from watching Sigerson-san work and one of the things I had learned was not discussing the solution to a problem until, as Sigerson-san put it, all the pieces of the puzzle were in place.

When we got to the Karuizawa jail we were once again ushered into the back to see Mr. Lock. He was sitting much as we left him but when he saw us return he stood up in great excitement and said, "Have you gentlemen brought me good news? Am I getting out of here?"

"That may depend on the answer to a question," I said.

"What is it?" he asked.

"When you heard Reverend Pearson talk, right before you heard his scream as he plunged down the cliff, was he speaking English or was he speaking Japanese?"

The next morning the air was a little cold but the sky was a clear blue. I sat in the study of Cloud Lodge watching the veranda through the open door in nervous anticipation. I thought I was correct in my deductions but the experiment that Sigerson-san had proposed would soon show if my chain of thought matched the reality of the situation.

I had been sitting for half an hour and my initial tension at the start of the experiment was slowly easing. Then I saw a reddish hand, covered in light-colored fur, grip the top of the railing. Immediately my body went taut.

The Japanese snow monkey hoisted himself up to the railing and sat for a few moments, looking about him with caution, his red face a study in concentration. He was large, about the size of a small child, and his face had watchful eyes. Then he quickly hopped down to the floor of the veranda and immediately leapt to the top of the table. There he reached for one of the fruits in the bowl on the table.

I suddenly jumped up from the desk and ran for the veranda, shouting "Saru!" The monkey leapt off the table, knocking some of the fruit in the bowl to the floor, and hopped to the veranda railing and over it.

I skidded to a stop at the veranda railing. I could easily see how Reverend Pearson, surprised and agitated by the sight of a Japanese snow monkey taking the precious pearl he so valued, could misjudge the distance and tumble over the rail to the rocks below.

I looked over the rail and saw the monkey scampering down the cliff, doing something no man could do without the help of ropes. I looked to the bottom of the cliff and I saw Mr. Short step out from behind a bush watching the path of the fleeing monkey. I knew that further down the slope Sigerson-san and Mr. MacKenzie were also waiting to track the path of the animal.

Within an hour all three gentlemen returned to Cloud Lodge and crowded into the small study.

"Were you successful?" I asked anxiously.

"More than successful." Sigerson-san took out something from his pocket and held it up for me to see. It was a large pink pearl dangling from a delicate gold chain. "I found it in the forest where the monkey dropped it. The beast took the same escape path he took last Tuesday when Reverend Pearson died. By following that path we were able to find the pearl."

"I am amazed at your success, Mr. Sigerson," Mr. Short said excitedly. "Can you explain how you knew what transpired with the death of Reverend Pearson?"

"Actually it was Doctor Watanabe who provided the key to this mystery. Perhaps he should explain his train of logic."

"It was nothing," I said. "Anyone who spoke Japanese could guess what happened."

"We are learning Japanese," Mr. Short said, "but we were not able to put together what happened."

"I'm sure with a little more study you would have, although I hope you never have to encounter a bizarre situation such as this one."

"But please explain things to us," Mr. MacKenzie begged. "I confess I am still very confused how you could decipher all that occurred."

"Well," I began, "it all started with what Mr. Lock heard as he ascended the stairs to talk to Reverend Pearson. He said he thought he heard Reverend Pearson saying 'don't' or 'go away.' At first I thought he was unsure because he couldn't hear Reverend Pearson clearly but as I waited here in the study as Sigerson-san examined the veranda I saw something that made me think Mr. Lock's uncertainty had another cause."

"What was that?" Mr. Short asked.

"In English the words don't or go away are really very different. Even if he couldn't hear them distinctly it would be unlikely that Mr. Lock could confuse the two. But in Japanese to leave, don't, and to go away can be the same word, saru. If Reverend Pearson was speaking Japanese then it would be very possible to confuse the meaning. However, saru has another meaning in Japanese, and the fact that Mr. Lock is not completely fluent in Japanese could mean that he wasn't aware of this meaning. Something in this room reminded me of that."

I picked up the carving of the three monkeys. "We call this carving the San-en. The original carving is at Toshogu Shrine in Nikko. The statue represents a kind of pun in Japanese. Saru in Japanese can mean don't and it also means monkey, so these three monkeys are Mizaru, don't see evil monkey, Iwazaru, don't say evil monkey, and Kikazaru, don't hear evil monkey. We just change the 's' in saru to a 'z' because we like the sound better but in this case we mean both don't and monkey when we say zaru."

"So Reverend Pearson was yelling at a snow monkey!" Mr. Short said.

"That's right," I said. "The Reverend was sitting at his desk and he happened to glance out at the veranda. There he saw a Japanese snow monkey that had climbed up on the veranda to steal some fruit. He noticed the monkey had picked up the pearl that he had left on the table. The startled monkey tried to flee and jumped to the railing, leaving some small scratches with his claws. Sigerson-san found the scratches.

"The Reverend, who saw his future retirement in that pearl, tried to pursue the beast. In his zeal to recapture his pearl he misjudged his momentum and tumbled over the railing to his death. Instead of murder the Reverend's death is a terrible accident. If Mr. Lock had followed the admonition of the three monkeys' statue and not spoken of what he heard, perhaps a fourth evil might have been perpetrated. By remaining silent about what he really heard, just to protect himself, Mr. Lock would have denied me the clue I needed to discover that he heard the word 'saru' as he entered the lodge. That would have been a miscarriage of justice. It certainly would have been the greatest of evils if an innocent man, no matter how self-righteous, was punished for a murder he did not commit."

The Adventure of the Purloined Pickles

Exotic foods don't

Remind me of my old home.

Give me a pickle!

"I suppose you are here about the jewels stolen a week ago," I said to Officer Suzuki.

He sighed. "No, Doctor, I am not. It seems that the case is too delicate for a country policeman such as me," he said with bitterness. "As you know, the jewels were stolen from Lady Petrushkin, a Russian aristocrat. The diplomatic situation between Russia and Japan is very delicate at this time so policemen from Tokyo were sent here to Karuizawa to handle the case."

"And how are they coming along?"

Officer Suzuki hung his head down miserably. "I don't know. They have completely excluded me from their investigation."

"So what can I help you with?" I asked.

"It's a silly matter. It happened around the same time as the jewel theft but to the victims involved it is a serious issue. It is a bizarre crime and I know how much you and your gaijin guest like this kind of mystery. Besides, to be truthful, it has puzzled me and if I can't work on the jewel theft I would at least like to solve this one."

"Let me see if Sigerson-san is interested in hearing about this crime although if it is, as you say, bizarre, I am sure he will be."

I excused myself and went upstairs. Before I could call Sigerson-san's name outside the shouji screen to his room he said, "Come in, Doctor." I had ceased being surprised about things like his knowing I was outside his room. I was sure he could tell it was me just from the sound of my footfall.

I opened the shouji and found Sigerson-san sitting on a pile of zabuton pillows, puffing on his pipe and wreathed in smoke. In his lap was the old Persian slipper he used to hold his tobacco—a custom that still repelled me. When I told him what Officer Suzuki said he immediately sprang to his feet.

"Capital, Doctor! Simply capital! I was running out of chess problems to solve in my head and Officer Suzuki's diversion couldn't come at a more opportune time."

We both went down to my parlor and, after the customary greetings, Officer Suzuki continued with me translating.

"Actually, now that I've had time to think about it, I feel foolish for bothering you with this," he started. "It's just such a strange crime that I'm completely baffled by it."

Sigerson-san held up a hand. "Please tell Officer Suzuki that I welcome the diversion of a strange problem. Besides, sometimes a small crime, especially an unusual one, can blossom into something more important."

Reassured, Officer Suzuki continued his tale.

"There's a shop in town run by the Kuroda family that sells a variety of foodstuffs. They sell rice, vegetables, and other goods but what they are known for in Karuizawa is the excellence of their homemade pickles. Their specialty is *takuan*."

"What's that?" Sigerson-san asked when I translated this part.

"Takuan is a pickle made from a dried radish. It's packed in rice bran and other ingredients and allowed to pickle for months. It is delicious but some people find the smell very potent," I explained.

"Please ask the Officer to continue."

"The Kurodas make their pickles for just the local market," Officer Suzuki said, "so it is not a big operation. They keep their pickle pots in the back of their shop in a small yard. Because it takes a few months for each batch to mature they rotate several batches with four to five pots in each batch.

"A few days ago the Kurodas awoke to find all the pickle pots in their back yard had been stolen. There were approximately twenty jars, and they were all gone. The money the Kurodas make from the pickles is not huge but it's important to a small family business like theirs. They not only lost the income those pickles represented, they also have the expense of buying new pots, rice bran and radishes if they want to start pickle production again.

"I do not understand why someone would go to the trouble of stealing so many pickles," Officer Suzuki said, "but last night something even more puzzling happened. The Kurodas live above their shop and they've been in a heightened state of alert ever since their pickles were stolen. They were sleeping when they heard a noise in their shop last night. They roused themselves and went downstairs to see what was happening. They couldn't make out his features but a man was in their shop. When he saw them he grabbed something from the shop and ran. You'll never guess what he stole."

I translated this for Sigerson-san. Officer Suzuki was taking Sigerson-san too lightly, I thought, because even I could guess what was stolen although I had no idea why.

"He took a jar of pickles," Sigerson-san said dryly.

The look on Officer Suzuki's face at this answer said he thought he had come to the right place to solve this mystery.

"This is a very interesting problem," Sigerson-san said. "Do you have the time to go to the Kurodas' shop, Doctor, to see the scene of this pickle theft?"

"I do."

"Good. Then if Officer Suzuki can accompany us there is no time like the present to go."

After a few minutes' walk we were in Karuizawa, in the back yard of the Kuroda shop. Kuroda came out to attend to us while his wife watched the store. He gave deep bows to Sigerson-san, Officer Suzuki, and me... a shopkeeper's bow, but sincere nonetheless.

The Kuroda shop was a typical two-story town shop, one room wide and set on a small lot. Most of the bottom floor was taken up by the shop. The living quarters were on the upper floor. In the back there was a small yard, a well, a toilet, and a vegetable garden.

"The vegetable garden is newly tilled," Sigerson-san said. "When did Mr. Kuroda create it?"

"Right before the theft of my pickles, Sensei-sama," Kuroda said to me after I translated. As a shopkeeper, he was used to appending the high honorific "sama" to everyone's name or title.

"Interesting," Sigerson-san said as he closely examined the ground next to the garden.

"Can Mr. Kuroda tell me how big his pickle jars are?" Sigerson-san asked.

Kuroda put his hands apart to show the size.

"I'm sorry," Sigerson-san said, "I can't quite picture how big these jars are. Does Mr. Kuroda have a sample of these jars he could show me?"

Kuroda thought a second, then said, "Can you tell the gaijin-sama that if he will wait a moment I can fetch a jar from our kitchen. It's the only jar of pickles we have left." After bowing Kuroda bustled off to get the jar. In a few moments he returned with a rough earthenware jar in his hands. The jar was the size of a large melon and the top was capped with oiled paper and twine.

Sigerson-san reached out and took the jar from the shopkeeper. "It would take a lot of effort to haul off twenty of these jars," Sigerson-san remarked. "Does Mr. Kuroda mind if I taste the pickles which seem worth stealing?" he asked.

Kuroda bowed and replied, "I would be honored if the gaijin-sama wants to try my humble pickles."

Sigerson-san peeled the paper cap off the jar and immediately recoiled. We Japanese are quite used to the smell but foreigners, especially foreigners with large beak-like noses like Sigerson-san, can have troubles with it.

I thought Sigerson-san was going to stop his experiment with Japanese pickle tasting but he plunged his hand into the jar and fished around for a pickle. "Excuse me," he said, "I have to wash the rice bran off my pickle before I eat it."

Sigerson-san went off to the well and took a bucket of water to wash off the pickle. In a few moments he returned holding a small takuan in his hand. He turned the pickled radish about, studying it like a crime scene. Then, to my great surprise, he took a small bite.

"Despite the smell it is actually quite tasty," he said. "Please tell Mr. Kuroda that I can see why his pickles are irresistible to thieves. In fact, instead of returning this jar of pickles to his kitchen, I believe we should put the jar on the counter in Mr. Kuroda's shop where it can be seen from the front window. I am sure it will lure the thief back to the scene of his crimes." Sigerson-san placed the oiled paper and string back on the top of the jar.

"Thank the gaijin-sama for his kind words about my pickles," Kuroda said, bewildered, "but...." The long pause indicated Kuroda's doubts about Sigerson-san's predictive ability.

"Surely no pickles are so delicious that they will tempt the thief back to this shop," Officer Suzuki said, expressing Kuroda's unspoken thought.

"I have had a chance to observe Sigerson-san in quite a few situations involving crime," I said. "I know it sounds like crazy henna gaijin talk, but he has never been wrong in his pronouncements about a criminal. Put the jar in the shop and let's see what develops."

Late that night Sigerson-san and I were crouching behind the counter in the Kuroda store. On the counter sat the jar of pickles. We'd been there for several hours and my legs were cramping and I was getting cold. Sigerson-san seemed oblivious to the discomfort and he waited patiently, like a stone Buddha. Suddenly we heard a rattling at the door to the shop. Then we heard some creaking as the crude lock on the door was forced.

I tensed up and waited for Sigerson-san to act. In my pocket I had a candle and some matches, but I wasn't sure my hands would be steady enough to light the candle. I was trembling with nervous energy. It's funny, on reflection, that I should be so excited about this situation. In my life I have had occasion to cut into another human being to perform a life-saving operation and I could do this surgery with absolute calm and concentration. But waiting in the darkened shop to spring at a thief had left me shaking and anxious.

Sigerson-san waited until the intruder was completely in the shop. Then he stood up. I followed his lead. As I stood I shouted, "Stop, thief!" I was glad to see my voice was steady even though my heart was pounding with excitement.

I expected the thief to flee immediately but he surprised me. He lunged towards us. At first I thought he was trying to attack us, perhaps with a knife, and I put my hands up, prepared to defend myself. Instead of striking us, however, he reached forward and snatched the jar of pickles from the counter! Only after he seized the pickles did he try to flee.

He spun around but by this time Officer Suzuki and Kuroda were blocking the shop door. Even in the darkened shop I could see the thief's shoulders sag. Unlike a cornered rat, which will fight, this man simply gave up. I took my time taking the candle from my pocket and lighting it.

The thief looked around him and seemed surprised at the sight of Sigerson-san. He was not expecting a gaijin. He was more surprised when Sigerson-san walked over to him and pried the pickle jar out of his hands.

Officer Suzuki went to the criminal and quickly and efficiently tied his hands. Officer Suzuki looked at me and said, "Please tell the gaijin-san that I am shocked that this man had such an uncontrollable desire for pickles."

In the flickering candlelight I could see Sigerson-san flash his brief smile. "Despite the undoubted flavor of the pickles that is not why the thief has been so insistent on stealing from this shop. He, in fact, has not been after the pickles. He has been after the jars."

"Why would he want the pickle jars?" Officer Suzuki asked.

"Because hidden in one of the jars were these." Sigerson-san reached into his pocket, withdrew his hand,

and opened it to show us what it held. In the flickering light of the candle we could see that Sigerson-san was holding a handful of sparkling jewels; rings, earrings, a bracelet, and a necklace. "I think you will find that these are the jewels stolen from Lady Petrushkin," Sigerson-san said.

The thief looked at the jewels with a combination of desire and anger. Officer Suzuki, Kuroda, and I all had expressions of astonishment on our faces.

"I found these in the pickle jar when I took it to the well to wash off the pickle," Sigerson-san said.

"How did they get in the jar?" Officer Suzuki gasped.

"There's a simple explanation," Sigerson-san said. "After stealing the jewels the thief tried to make good his escape. Was there a pursuit of this man after the theft?"

"There was," Officer Suzuki said.

"The pursuers must have come close to apprehending him, then," Sigerson-san said. "During the pursuit the thief passed the back yard of this shop. He was afraid he would be caught with the jewels on him so he decided to temporarily hide them. He saw the pickle jars in the back yard and decided that putting the jewels in the rice bran that covered the pickles would be a perfect hiding place. He knew that it takes a considerable amount of time to make these pickles so he felt safe they would be secure for a day or two, until he could return to retrieve them. What he didn't anticipate was that the jars might be moved in the interim. When Mr. Kuroda created his back yard garden he moved the pickle jars to one side of the yard."

"That's right," Kuroda said when I translated this. "How did he know?"

"I could see the outline of the jars in the soil. It was plain that they had recently been shuffled around. Add that to the newness of the garden and it was not necessary to ask Mr. Kuroda if they had been moved. When Mr. Kuroda moved the jars he took one into his kitchen for the personal consumption of his family. Unfortunately for the thief, that jar held the jewels.

"When the thief came back to retrieve the jewels he could no longer discern which jar was the one he used to hide the jewels. Therefore, in the dead of night, he decided it was faster to simply steal all the jars instead of conducting a search in the back yard of the shop. One can imagine his disappointment when none of the jars had the jewels. That's why he came back and stole the pickle jars in the shop. He didn't know there was an additional jar of pickles in the Kuroda kitchen.

"At his wits' end, he must have viewed the appearance of a new jar of pickles in the shop as a godsend. That's why he risked coming back to steal it."

"This is the cleverest gaijin I've ever met," Officer Suzuki said with admiration. He bowed deeply to Sigerson-san. Sigerson-san started to bow back but I raised my hand to stop him. Officer Suzuki was showing his respect for Sigerson-san and it would not be appropriate for Sigerson-san to match his bow. Seeing my gesture, Sigerson-san merely nodded to acknowledge the bow from Officer Suzuki, which was a suitable response.

"I'm sorry that my colleagues from Tokyo will be upset that a gaijin solved the case of the jewel theft," Officer Suzuki said. The smile on his face didn't make it look like he was sorry.

"Actually, I would appreciate it if you minimize my involvement," Sigerson-san said. I understood what he meant. It wouldn't do for him to become too famous, especially with people from Tokyo.

"But there's a reward," Officer Suzuki protested. "Sigerson-san should get it."

"I think the Kurodas should get some of the reward," Sigerson-san said, "to compensate them for their lost business and the expense of getting their pickle manufacturing going again. If any money is left over I am sure that Officer Suzuki knows of some local charities that can benefit from it."

Kuroda bowed when he heard Sigerson-san's generous division of the reward. "But surely the gaijin-sama should get something for his efforts!" Kuroda said.

Sigerson-san heard my translation of this, paused a moment, then held up the last jar of pickles. "Then I will take this, with Mr. Kuroda's permission. Despite their pungent odor, I was serious when I said they were actually quite excellent pickles."

The Adventure of the White Threads

A curtain of white

Opens to reveal the past.

A samurai ghost.

"Do you have some cocaine, Doctor?"

I looked up in surprise. I had just finished with the patients in my surgery and was cleaning up for the day. Takada-san had made another of her "visits" and I was a bit irritated. Her desire to have a formal *miai*, a marriage meeting, between her daughter and me was bordering on obsession and I was getting tired of it. Sigerson-san almost never intruded on my work so it was unusual to see him at my surgery door. In his hand he had a compact brown case of Moroccan leather. It was open and inside the case I could see a syringe, some hypodermic needles and a glass vial.

"Why do you ask that, Sigerson-san?"

He took the vial from the case and held it up. "I am completely out," he said. "I have been away from Europe for quite some time and I have used up my supply of cocaine. I prefer a seven-percent solution, if you have it."

I looked at Sigerson-san and asked, "Is there a medical reason you are taking cocaine?" I knew that Western doctors often prescribed cocaine as a tonic but this was one part of Dutch Medicine that I was a bit leery of. Dutch Medicine places great store in drugs, just as Chinese Medicine places great store in herbs. However, I've noticed that patients can become quite dependent on things like cocaine or laudanum and I wasn't sure that taking anything without a good reason was sound.

"Actually, Doctor, I use it to relieve my boredom," Sigerson-san said.

"Boredom?"

"Yes. Things have been very quiet for the last few days and I have explored all the areas surrounding your house. When I came here Colonel Ashworth and I agreed that I should visit the town sparingly so things have been a bit boring."

I was stunned. I did not have a mind as agile as Sigerson-san but I was fascinated the entire time I was in London. Everything was so new and interesting to me. Here it was Sigerson-san's first time in Japan and, because we hadn't recently had the kind of crime that seemed to fascinate him, he was bored! I was speechless but Sigerson-san didn't seem to notice my reaction.

"So do you have any cocaine?" His eyes bored into mine and I thought that here was a man who seemed a bit desperate to obtain the drug. That concerned me more than Sigerson-san's confession that he was bored.

I found my voice. "No, Sigerson-san, I don't. But if you are bored I suggest we make a small outing. It is Friday and my normal surgery hours are finished for the week. I'll tell Hosokawa-san where we are going in case there is an emergency and you and I will take a short hike to Shiraito Falls. We can get there before nightfall if we start immediately. We can spend the weekend there at one of the teahouses at the foot of the falls. I'm sure the new scenery will stimulate you and dispel your boredom."

Sigerson-san didn't look totally convinced at my prescription, but since I didn't have the cocaine he desired he resigned himself to accompany me on the proposed adventure. Within twenty minutes I had told Hosokawa-san where we were going, filled a knapsack with some essentials like my razor and some spare clothes, put on my hiking shoes, got my hiking stick, and was leading Sigerson-san out my front door.

My expectation was that an experienced explorer would like to plan trips out carefully but Sigerson-san was energized by the sudden activity. He seemed to enjoy the spontaneous action and his eyes lit up with a suppressed excitement.

As we left the house Hosokawa-san came running after us, saying, *"Shoushou omachi kudasai,* Sensei!" In her hands was a *furoshiki* and I knew immediately why she asked me to wait a minute. Inside the furoshiki, the ubiquitous cloth bundle we Japanese use to carry things, was undoubtedly food. Knowing Hosokawa-san, it was surely delicately prepared and in a quantity more suited to an expedition to China than a weekend trip to Shiraito Falls. I, of course, thanked her profusely for her trouble.

Then, holding the furoshiki in one hand and the hiking stick in the other, I started on our journey again with Sigerson-san walking beside me.

As we walked away from my house I thought that this excursion would probably do as much good for me as for Sigerson-san. I had no serious cases pending and Hosokawa-san could always send a messenger for me if there was an emergency. The chance to get back in close proximity to nature was something I needed but didn't realize. We Japanese have always lived as part of the natural world. Our houses are designed to open up to nature by sliding back screens. We still place as much emphasis on our gardens as we do on the décor of our reception rooms. Our festivals, by and large, are attuned to the changing seasons, as is our diet. We have great delight in the tastes of a new season. Nothing is as good as the first *takenoko*, bamboo shoots, of the season or perhaps the first *ayu*, sweetfish, from the river.

My musings about our culture were quickly forgotten as I immersed myself in the sheer joy of my surroundings. The birds flitted between the trees and the sunlight filtered through the branches forming golden rays like the bamboo ribs of a fan. Even Sigerson-san seemed to enjoy the walk as we wandered further away from my house and towards the trail that led from Karuizawa to Shiraito Falls.

Sigerson-san was not what I would call a talkative man. When he did talk it was usually something insightful based on his observations but he was not one who usually made idle chatter. In this way he was difficult to get to know well because the small bits of a man's life—his schooling, home life, past experiences—are often revealed as part of daily conversation that otherwise has no meaning.

Despite his long silences I found him a companionable hiking partner. He took the knapsack from me and walked beside me when the path was wide enough. He had the long, loping stride of a tall man used to walking. I was much shorter than him and I have the typical long torso and short legs that mark the Japanese body type but I was still able to keep up with him because I was used to walking fast.

We made good time, invigorated by the beauty around us, and soon reached the main road to Shiraito Falls just as dusk was falling. Walking on the rough dirt road was not as pleasant as the path in the forest but we only had to go a short distance before we came to a small cluster of teahouses and shops that stood near Shiraito Falls. "We'll spend the night here in one of the teahouses," I told Sigerson-san, "then we'll go on to the falls tomorrow morning." Sigerson-san nodded.

As we approached the teahouses a man came running from one of the houses towards us. He started bowing and said, "Hello gentlemen! Hello!" If he was surprised by the sight of Sigerson-san he didn't show it.

Many gaijin tourists came to see the falls so someone of Sigerson-san's height and race wouldn't be totally unusual. "Are you looking to stay the night? I have the finest teahouse in the village. Please stay at my place! You will be most welcome!" He gave us an insincere smile that could be seen even in the gathering gloom of evening.

"What is he asking us?" Sigerson-san said.

"He wants us to stay the night at his teahouse."

Sigerson-san judged him with his keen eye and said, "There might be better places to stay in this village."

"I agree. He reminds me of a Kyoto merchant: All smiles and friendly greetings when he is trying to get your money but full of harsh words and contempt as soon as you are out of earshot. Osaka merchants are almost as bad, only interested in commerce and turning a business arrangement solely to their advantage. Only Tokyo merchants are both sincere and honest."

"I see your family is from the Tokyo area."

I had never spoken of my family before and said, "How did you know...." Then I stopped. It didn't require the abilities of Sigerson-san to interpret my remarks into an understanding that my family was from the Tokyo area. I started to laugh and he gave a small smile.

The teahouse owner misinterpreted this sign of mirth. "Ah," he said, "You gentlemen will enjoy my hospitality! For a small extra fee I can even provide you with some female companionship. My maid is very pretty and young." He pointed to his teahouse. There I could see two women. One was middle-aged with unruly hair and a greedy, feral look to her face. The other was younger but she looked as skinny as an underfed dog and her pinched face had dirt smudges. I wasn't quite sure which one he was offering to us but a man would have to be indiscriminate and desperate to want to spend time with either one of them. He smiled apologetically. "Of course there will be an extra fee if the gaijin wants companionship, too," he said.

I looked at the teahouse owner and said coldly, "We will stay at another teahouse."

The man looked surprised and said, "But I will offer you a big discount! You must stay with me. The other teahouses here are miserable and infected with fleas!"

"That's not true, Higashi!" a female voice said. From out of the twilight darkness we could see an older woman approach us. She was wearing a kimono and apron and she bowed to us as she approached.

"There are five teahouses in this little village, gentlemen," she said. "Four of them will give you a nice meal and a clean place to sleep for a fair price. Pick any of them and you will have a pleasant stay before you go to see the falls tomorrow." She bowed again. "I'm sorry to say this but Higashi says bad things about his competitors and exaggerates the virtues of his own teahouse. Unless you gentlemen are looking for a certain type of vice, if I may be so bold as to say, you will be more comfortable in any of the other establishments in our little village."

"Get out of here, you old hag!" Higashi shouted.

"What's happening?" Sigerson-san said. I quickly informed him of the situation leaving out the part about the offer of the maid. I knew London, and I assume the rest of Europe, had women of easy virtue but frankly this was not a topic I wished to discuss with another gentleman. As I explained to Sigerson-san, the two continued to argue.

"Please don't call me names, Higashi," the woman said. "You might have the most money in this village but that doesn't give you the right to insult people. The gentlemen deserve to know there are other places to stay in this village and that your remarks about the rest of us are not true. Besides, since when has it been the custom of our village to try and steal customers even before they enter the village?"

The man turned to us and whined, "Don't listen to her. She is simply a troublemaker! Come to my teahouse. The *sake* is warm and the maid will spend time with your gaijin friend with no premium charge."

My jaw tightened and I asked the woman, "What is your name?"

"I am Okada, sir. I own that teahouse over there."

"We will spend the night at your teahouse, Okada."

"Thank you, sir! We will do our best to make you comfortable!"

To the protests of Higashi, Sigerson-san and I followed Okada to her teahouse. Once at the teahouse we were shown to a clean room and Okada immediately brought us tea so we could relax. I opened the furoshiki and found a lacquered box with a *Kamakura-bori* cherry blossom design. I took off the deeply carved top and examined the food inside. There were a variety of rice balls, either covered with seaweed or stuffed with various salty pickles. There was some *oden* stew in a separate compartment in the box and another compartment had some grilled fish on skewers. My mouth started watering at the sight.

Hosokawa-san had put *hashi*, chopsticks, in the box. Thoughtfully, she had also included a fork for Sigerson-san. Not so thoughtfully, I saw a pat of butter was also included. It was obvious that Hosokawa-san was still not won over by Sigerson-san. Still, the sight of the food was delightful and I started eating hungrily. Sigerson-san picked listlessly at the food, eating some of the stew.

"You don't like Japanese food, do you, Sigerson-san?"

"Frankly I would prefer a nice piece of mutton or beef," he said.

"I'm afraid you will only find something like that at certain hotels in Tokyo or perhaps at the Mampei. Cows and sheep are rather rare here in Japan."

Okada came to the room to see if we needed dinner but when she saw what Hosokawa-san had packed for us she remarked that we were already well taken care of. She did, however, bring us tea after we refused the offer of sake.

When we finished Okada set out clean bedding for us and we went to sleep. Just before we drifted off I could hear the rumbling of hunger pains in Sigerson-san's stomach. Sigerson-san was already thin and gaunt when I met him but I vowed to keep an eye on him to make sure he didn't waste away for lack of nutrition.

The next morning Okada offered her son Jiro as a guide for us. Living in Karuizawa I had been to Shiraito Falls before but thought it would be nice to have a guide. Jiro was a lad of around eighteen with a round face, a ready smile and a pleasant nature. The trail from the little village to the falls was an easy one and we were able to walk in just a few minutes.

"Is there construction going on by the falls?" Sigerson-san asked.

When I asked Jiro he nodded in the affirmative. "Higashi wants to build a teahouse right next to the falls," he said. "My mother and the other teahouse owners are against it but Higashi doesn't listen. His teahouse will hurt the business for everyone else. No one else has built by the falls because they don't want to spoil the beauty but Higashi doesn't care. He is so selfish!"

I explained the situation to Sigerson-san who then asked, "Was any workman injured?"

I found this a surprising question but when I asked it, Jiro said, "No. Not really…"

It was plain from the way his voice trailed off that Jiro had something on his mind so I asked another question to draw out his thoughts. "Will the village do anything about the building of a teahouse at the falls? I would not like Shiraito Falls spoiled by a building up there."

"Construction has stopped," Jiro said.

"Why?"

He hesitated again. "Well…"

"Well what? Come on, young man, speak up!"

"The ghosts are protecting the falls."

"Ghosts?"

Jiro looked at me nervously. "My mother told me not to talk about it because it will drive customers away."

I tried to show patience. Sometimes a patient is reluctant to tell you exactly what is wrong with them, either through embarrassment or nervousness, so you must draw the story out of them. Jiro was like a reluctant patient.

"But we are already here," I pointed out, "so telling us would not discourage us. Besides you are supposed to be our guide and a guide must tell interesting stories about the places visited. Surely a story about ghosts is interesting."

Jiro considered this a moment. "Will you tell my mother I told you?"

"Of course not."

He took a deep breath, "There are ghosts of ancient samurai protecting the falls."

"How?"

"When Higashi sent workmen to the falls the ghosts appeared and scared the workmen away."

I translated all this for Sigerson-san and his face immediately took on a look of keen interest. "Ask him for details about the ghosts," he requested.

Jiro dropped his voice to a conspiratorial whisper even though we three were alone on the path. "There were two ancient samurai," he said. "They were dressed in armor and had helmets. The workmen said the ghosts had truly frightening faces. They waved their swords at the workmen and told them to flee. The workmen were so scared they ran all the way down to the village. Those were tough guys but they were pale and shaking."

"Interesting," I said. "Aren't you frightened taking us to the falls?"

"No," Jiro said with more certainty than he must have felt. "We never heard of ghosts at the falls until Higashi's workmen started construction. The ghosts came to protect the falls from Higashi's building. They won't harm anyone who is coming to the falls just to see its beauty. At least that's what my mother told me. Besides, my mother gave me a charm against the ghosts." He extracted a small cloth charm, the kind you buy at local shrines for a few *sen*, and showed it to me.

"When did these ghosts appear?" I asked.

"Just a few days ago. Workmen from around here won't work at the falls anymore but Higashi says he will get workmen from outside the area and finish his teahouse."

I told Sigerson-san what Jiro said. Sigerson-san seemed deep in thought but he asked no more questions as we made our way to the falls.

If you have not visited it, you should know that Shiraito Falls is a rather unique waterfall. Most spectacular waterfalls plunge from a great height or involve a huge volume of water. Shiraito is impressive for another reason.

Picture a rough-edged cliff in the shape of a large crescent. The cliff has a sheer face of sharp gray rock, tufted with green patches, and extending about twice the height of a man. From the face of the cliff, starting at the top, numerous white threads of water emerge from the cliff face and plunge down to a clear pool at the base. The effect is a wide, curved curtain of water made up of individual white threads which is why we call it Shiraito ("White Threads") Falls.

I stood enjoying the sight but noticed that Sigerson-san was looking around him surveying the land surrounding the falls and not looking at the falls itself. "Don't you enjoy waterfalls?" I asked.

"Not particularly," he said. "I had a close call at a waterfall and I almost died. In fact, another man did die."

"I'm sorry to hear that," I said.

"Don't be," he replied. "The world is a better place because that man died."

I had already learned not to press Sigerson-san for details he was not willing to volunteer no matter how tantalizing his remarks might be. Besides, I frankly tend to agree that the world is often a better place when certain people pass to the void.

Sigerson-san continued to look around him.

"What are you looking for?" I asked.

"Can you ask the boy where the workmen saw the ghosts?" Sigerson-san sometimes had the irritating habit of asking another question instead of answering one. Regardless, I did as he requested.

Jiro pointed to the top of the falls, to an area near the edge where water was emerging. "I think it was there," he said. "I didn't see the ghosts myself but that's where the workmen said they saw them."

Sigerson-san needed no translation. He looked at the top of the falls where Jiro had indicated and studied the area carefully. "So the warrior ghosts were at the top of the cliff and not near us?" Sigerson-san asked.

When I conveyed the question to Jiro he said, "*Hai.* Yes. At least I think so."

"Why is that important?" I asked Sigerson-san.

He walked a short distance from us and pointed. "Because of this," he said.

I walked over to see what he was pointing at and Jiro followed. As soon as Jiro saw what was on the ground he let out a shout of fear and immediately started running down the path towards the village. As he ran I could glimpse the cloth charm clutched tightly in his hand.

Just off the path, hidden slightly by a boulder, was the bloody body of a man.

As a doctor I do not find the sight of a cadaver frightening, although I could understand why Jiro did. The dead man was the innkeeper Higashi and there is a greater horror of violent death when you know the victim. And this was a violent death. Very violent. I took a quick glance at Sigerson-san and found him unflappable with an unnerving detachment in his gaze.

I moved forward to examine the body and Sigerson-san placed his arm out to stop me. "Please, Doctor, let me examine the area around the body before you examine him. It's plain that Higashi is no longer in a condition where medical attention may be beneficial."

Sigerson-san was right. Higashi was sprawled on his back. There was a long gash that extended from the right side of Higashi's neck and down to his breastbone. From the depth of the wound, the length of the jagged cut, the gaping flesh, and the amount of blood on his kimono, it was plain that there was no helping Higashi. Strangely, there was postmortem lividity on the left side of his face even though the body was lying on its back. Sigerson-san was right: There was nothing I could do that would make any difference to Higashi.

Sigerson-san started his now familiar ritual of inspecting the crime scene. He circled the body like a bear, searching for irregularities in the rocky ground around Higashi's body. He dropped to his knees a couple of times, placing his head low to the ground so he could use a different angle to help him perceive changes to the soil which would give him clues about how Higashi's body came to be by the falls.

During this entire process Sigerson-san's face was a study in concentration. But I detected something else. Sometimes gaijin are painfully obvious as emotions flit across their face. It's like a child, not a proper adult who has been trained to politely keep their emotions to themselves. Other times gaijin can be totally inscrutable, or perhaps we Japanese just can't pick up the subtle clues that could tell us what they are thinking. By and large Sigerson-san fell into the latter group and his emotions were kept to himself. It's what the British call a 'stiff upper lip'—although I don't know why. But now I had seen Sigerson-san investigate a crime site several times and this activity obviously energized and excited him.

His face displayed intense concentration but in his eyes there was a kind of spark. Sigerson-san seemed to be a man who was bored with the daily routine of life. However, when confronted with something dramatic, such as a crime, he became electric and his brain started functioning in a higher state; taking in, classifying, and analyzing observations at a prodigious rate. Even though our beautiful trip was now interrupted by a horrendous murder, Sigerson-san seemed truly happy for the first time in days. It was as if crime was his true drug and he used the cocaine he wanted from me as a poor substitute. This disturbed me and made me wonder about the hidden character of the man now closely examining the crime scene.

Finally he stood and said, "This site will tell us no more. Unfortunately it is very rocky here and therefore the evidence I can glean is less than I hoped."

"Did you discover anything at all?" I asked.

Before Sigerson-san could answer we heard excited voices coming up the path from the village. "Any additional evidence the path might yield is being erased from the sound of it. It seems to be the whole village is coming," he added.

Jiro must have flown down the path like the wind. It was only a short distance from the village to the falls but I would not have expected the villagers to appear so quickly. In seconds a crowd rounded a curve in the path. When they saw us they seemed to quicken their pace. In the front of the crowd were Jiro, his mother Okada, and the older woman I saw in Higashi's teahouse. As they came closer I realized that the older woman's face was not marked by dirt, as I thought when I first saw her the previous day. The duskiness on her face was bruises.

"Where is the body, Jiro?" Okada said. Since Sigerson-san and I were standing directly in front of the body that seemed like a superfluous thing to ask but in moments of high drama people usually say the obvious. Jiro came towards us tentatively and, when he did get the barest glimpse of the body, he pointed behind the rock that hid the corpse.

Naturally the entire crowd surged forward to get a look. Eyes widened with surprise, jaws dropped, and the bruised woman (whom I took to be Higashi's wife) covered her face with her hands. "He really is dead," Okada said in shock, almost as if she did not believe what her son had reported to the village. The crowd stood in silence staring at the body of Higashi. Then, from the back of the crowd, someone said, "It must have been the ghosts." Someone else took up the call. "Yes, the ghosts that protect the falls must have done it. It was a judgment from heaven." Like the typhoon rains which burst forth suddenly and pelt the earth, the conversation about the ghosts at the falls spilled forth from the crowd.

I looked at Sigerson-san. Raising his voice so it could be heard above the crowd he said, "It's not likely that we will learn any more here, Doctor. I suggest we return to the village and wait until the villagers have calmed sufficiently for us to ask a few more questions."

I nodded my agreement and Sigerson-san and I walked down the path from the falls to the village. Behind us the excited crowd remained.

"The villagers seemed very excited before we left," Sigerson-san remarked.

"Yes. Several thought Higashi was killed by the ghostly samurai that guard the falls."

"Fascinating. You've told me that most Japanese believe in ghosts but it's interesting that the village would think that the murder was committed by ghosts."

He didn't comment further nor did he ask me for my opinions about the body of Higashi. Halfway down the path it occurred to me that Sigerson-san had spent more time and attention looking at the body of Higashi than he spent enjoying the natural beauty of Shiraito Falls. I don't know if he found "beauty" in such a morbid sight but I did know that his brain, which just yesterday was so idle that he was seeking drugs to stimulate it, was now fully engaged.

We waited at the village for the inhabitants to return. It was strangely peaceful in the quiet village but Sigerson-san didn't take the time to relax. Instead, he drew from his pocket a pipe and that awful Persian type slipper where he kept his tobacco. He proceeded to fill his pipe and he sat on the porch of the teahouse smoking and thinking.

Presently the villagers straggled back from the falls. They saw me sitting on the porch with Sigerson-san and came towards me like a flock of ducks surging towards grain. Okada asked me, "What should we do, Sensei?"

At first I thought that question was a little ridiculous. I was a total stranger and a doctor, not a law enforcement officer. But then I realized that a small village like this probably had very little crime. A village like this was used to dispensing justice in its own way. If they caught a thief or someone else who was disrupting the harmony of the village they could punish them by ostracizing them or making their lives in the village miserable. When faced with a murder, however, the villagers were uncertain about what course of action to take. That is why they asked me, who was, I suppose, a symbol of some kind of outside authority.

"Someone must go to Karuizawa and ask for the policeman to come here," I said. "The policeman is Officer Suzuki." I didn't bother to pull out my pocket watch. Instead, I did what man has always done and looked at the sun in the sky. "If someone leaves right now he can get to Karuizawa by mid-afternoon, but it's unlikely he'll be able to find Officer Suzuki and return here today. If Officer

Suzuki won't be here until tomorrow morning then someone has to guard the body of Higashi. It's important that the body is not disturbed so that Officer Suzuki can see things for himself."

My pronouncement caused a great deal of excitement and conversation amongst the villagers. "What are they saying?" Sigerson-san asked.

"I told them someone has to protect the body but they are reluctant to do so. They believe ghosts killed Higashi. They fear that if they stay by the falls the ghosts of the two samurai the workmen saw will return and kill them. Some even think that the ghost of Higashi might return because ghosts are often related to a violent death. No one wants to go and protect the body."

"I don't know if that policeman will be able to read all the clues presented to him by that body," Sigerson-san said. "Still, you are right, Doctor. The body must be guarded so that the policeman can see for himself the evidence associated with the body. I don't know if you are prepared to spend a night under the stars, Doctor, but the weather is pleasant and sleeping outside tonight would not be too much of a hardship. If you agree I propose that we tell the villagers that we will guard the body."

I assented to Sigerson-san's proposal and told the villagers. Our offer was met with a mixture of relief, surprise, and fear for our safety. Since no one wanted to take our place, however, our offer was accepted.

Okada's son Jiro was sent to Karuizawa to inform Officer Suzuki of the murder but life in the village did not return to normal. Eventually the crowd dispersed and people returned to their businesses and homes. Through this commotion Sigerson-san sat smoking his pipe on the porch of Okada's teahouse, deep in thought and immobile as a stone Buddha. Quite suddenly he stood up, knocked the ashes from his pipe against the porch post, and said,

"Can we walk about the village before we go back to the falls, Doctor?"

I was shocked. One remarkable thing about Sigerson-san was his apparent lack of curiosity about Japanese culture and life. Unless it had to do with solving one of the crimes we had encountered he seemed to be oblivious to the fact he was living in another culture and country. I have seen this attitude amongst other gaijin, especially the missionaries in Tokyo and Yokohama, who seem most intent on creating a comfortable little world as much like their home country as possible. Many of these people, of course, are my patients as they flee the summer heat for the mountain air of Karuizawa, but I still find it strange that they would travel literally halfway around the world only to create a cloistered version of the life they left. Despite the fact that he was an explorer I had decided that Sigerson-san was of this temperament so I was surprised by his request.

Still wondering about Sigerson-san's sudden interest in Japanese village life, I took him for a walk. The village was not a typical country place. It was not centered on agriculture or some shrine or temple as most are but was instead devoted to catering to those visiting Shiraito Falls. It had five teahouses that also acted as inns plus several booths that sold rice crackers, roasted river fish on skewers, and similar snacks. It also had a few shops that sold various kinds of souvenirs to visitors, such as carved wooden trays or other gifts. It was one of these souvenir shops that captured Sigerson-san's attention.

The shop specialized in things made out of paper. The proprietor was a gentleman in his late fifties named Igarashi. He bowed to us politely as we entered the shop and gave us a cheerful *"Irasshaimase! Igarashi desu."*

Of course a shopkeeper who works with paper is as common as one who works with bamboo, but Igarashi was a true master at making things. In addition to the usual paper boxes and paper dolls, Igarashi was able to form the paper into masks, whimsical hats, and even little animals. When we entered his shop he was skillfully painting a child's kite with an image of Yoshitomo, complete with details of his armor and his prancing horse. Igarashi had an ability to make this ancient samurai hero come alive and you could see each metal scale of Yoshitomo's decorative armor cunningly painted so it looked like it was reflecting sunlight.

Sigerson-san walked over to Igarashi and observed his painting for a moment. "Could you tell the shopkeeper that I admire his skill?" Sigerson-san asked.

I did so and Igarashi bowed deeply in gratitude. "Could you continue to translate for me, Doctor? I would like to ask the shopkeeper some questions about his trade."

Later that afternoon we were back at the falls. Higashi's body was covered by an old tatami mat that the villagers had given us. Sigerson-san and I had set up a camp nearby. We sat on newer tatami mats and had quilts, water, and food that the villagers gave us. It would be a very pleasant way to spend an evening under the stars, assuming you were not bothered by a blood-soaked corpse only a few steps away.

I sat on the mat in proper fashion but Sigerson-san was indolently reclining in that manner that gaijin have. Even if you couldn't see our faces, from a distance you could easily tell that one of us was Japanese and the other was a foreigner just from our posture.

"The sun has just gone down and twilight is upon us," Sigerson-san remarked. Then, just as he finished his observation he sat upright and looked down the trail. "And here are our guests being delivered to us in a very punctual fashion."

I glanced down the trail and saw Okada bringing Higashi's widow and maid to us. To eliminate the necessary delays caused by translation Sigerson-san had coached me about what to say and I went through his instructions one more time in my mind. I was used to questioning patients about health concerns and their health history but this was an interview of an entirely different type.

"They didn't want to come," Okada said as they reached us, "but I told them they didn't have a choice. You demanded it and it was only proper. You are guarding Higashi's body to protect it from animals or evil spirits and they owe proper respect to you for that, Sensei."

"Why were you reluctant to come here?" I asked Higashi's wife.

"Because, Sensei, I was afraid of the ghosts that haunt this place. After all they killed my husband!" She put her face in her hands. Her shoulders shook in a piteous way and a few doubts entered my mind. Yet Sigerson-san had explained everything to me and I knew that if Higashi's wife had real tears they were not tears of remorse.

I tried to keep the sarcasm out of my voice as I said, "I can see why you might fear this place. But not for the reason you said. Do you know that ghosts are often interested in revenge if they are falsely accused of murder?"

The maid looked about her fearfully but Higashi's wife instantly stopped her show of tears, glared at me, and said to me rather insolently, "What do you mean?"

I stared at her for several long moments. The light was turning gray but even in the gathering gloom of twilight she could see the look on my face. She dropped her eyes and bowed several times rapidly. "*Gomen nasai*, Sensei. I am sorry. Please forgive my behavior. It's because I am upset about my husband and afraid of ghosts."

"I'm not sure you are upset about your husband at all. However you do have reason to fear the ghosts of this place. As I said, ghosts will take revenge if they are falsely accused of a murder."

Higashi's wife became wary and said, "What do you mean, Sensei?"

"My gaijin friend is a famous explorer and he is very good at observing things. When we came up to the falls this morning he noticed a handcart had been recently pulled up the path. He could see the ruts in the fresh dirt of the path covering previous footprints. He asked if construction was going on at the falls because he had seen handcarts used in Japan for construction projects. That's when we learned about the ghosts that inhabit the falls and your husband's plans to build a teahouse here. But we were told that the local workmen were scared away by the ghosts and no construction was going on here. But my friend is very curious and he wondered why a handcart was recently pulled all the way up the path if it wasn't used to bring construction materials to the falls. His curiosity was increased when he saw what he thought were blood drops on the trail, especially since he was told no workman was injured at the construction site.

"I know that construction is very costly," I continued. "It's a big debt for teahouse owners like you and your husband. The villagers told me that you borrowed money to start the construction here at the falls and that your husband was going to borrow even more money to get new workers who would work here and finish the construction of your new teahouse. His determination to borrow more money must have been a cause for fights between you and your husband. In fact the bruises on your face show your husband was so determined to have his way that he beat you." Higashi's wife involuntarily touched her face.

"Yes, we fought. What couple doesn't fight? And yes, my husband beat me but that's not uncommon, is it? My husband was killed by ghosts. Right here at the falls the samurai ghosts cut him with their swords."

"A sword makes a long, clean cut," I said. "The wound on your husband is jagged. He was not killed by a sword. He was killed by a knife."

"The ghosts of the falls killed him when he came to inspect the construction site," Higashi's wife said stubbornly.

"He wasn't even killed here." Both the wife and the maid looked at me with wide eyes.

"How do you know that, Sensei?" the maid said breathlessly.

"I can tell Higashi was lying on his side a long time. I know that from the pattern of blood stains on his kimono and the fact that blood pooled in his cheek. It takes hours for that to happen. As a doctor I saw that immediately. Even my gaijin friend noticed it. The body was lying on its back when it was found and the ground around the body was not soaked with blood."

Higashi's wife and the maid were silent now, looking at me warily.

"I will tell you exactly what happened," I said finally. "Higashi was killed in a fight with you," I said to Higashi's wife. "He may have been beating you or you may have feared he would beat you again. Regardless, you slashed at him with a knife, cutting deeply into his flesh, and he fell on his side, dying almost immediately. You let him stay like that until night fell and darkness hid your movements. You got one of the carts your husband had gathered for construction at the falls and had your maid help you load the body onto the cart. Then the two of you pulled the cart up to the falls and dumped the body here.

You were hoping that people would believe he was killed by the samurai ghosts guarding Shiraito Falls."

"But the ghosts did kill him!" Higashi's wife screamed, thinking that the volume of her protestations would make them more believable.

"That's a dangerous thing to say," I warned. "I told you ghosts do not like being falsely accused by mortals. They take revenge on liars." I looked past Higashi's wife and the maid at the path behind them. I raised my arm and pointed a finger down the path behind them. "Look! Here are the ghosts to punish you for your lies."

Higashi's wife and the maid spun around and looked down the path. There, in the gathering gloom of twilight, two ancient samurai warriors stood blocking the path to the village.

The warriors wore the traditional helmets of samurai generals. On the front of one helmet was a large brass crescent. On the other was a stylized deer antler. These were used to allow for easy identification on the battlefield. The helmets had large metal flaps that hung down to protect the necks of the samurai and on their faces the samurai had metal battle masks. The masks were designed to protect the face from swords and arrows but in the darkness the fearsome expressions of the metal masks made the faces of the ghostly apparitions even more frightening. On their bodies they wore the ancient plated armor of the samurai, each of the metal plates shining with oil and held to its neighboring plate with colorful cords. The gloved hands of the ghosts held shining *katana*, the traditional swords of the samurai.

The two women started at the sight of the ghosts and the maid gave a low moan and collapsed to her knees. "It's true! It's true!" the maid said. "The mistress killed the master in a fight and we hauled his body to the falls." She bowed to the ghosts putting her forehead on the grounds.

"Please forgive me, samurai-samas! The mistress wanted the village to believe ghosts killed the master. I just followed her orders. Please forgive me!"

I looked at Okada, who was very pale and trembling. Then I turned to Sigerson-san and took the opportunity to quickly update him on what transpired.

As I talked to Sigerson-san the two ghosts came closer. Higashi's wife, who had up to now shown a remarkable amount of courage in the face of the ghostly intruders, shrunk away from the advancing samurai. I could see her trembling with fear.

One of the samurai pulled the helmet off his head. Then he took off the battle mask. As he did so Higashi's wife gave a gasp of surprise. It was one of the other teashop owners in the village. The scene was repeated as the other ghost also removed his helmet and mask revealing Igarashi, the paper craftsman.

Okada was stunned by the unmasking of the ghosts. "Why are you dressed like that?" she blurted out.

"To scare the workmen Higashi hired to build up here," Igarashi said. "We knew he was intent on destroying the tranquility of the falls so we decided this was the way to stop any construction. We knew all this talk about ghosts killing Higashi was nonsense but we didn't want to reveal our deception. We were afraid we might be accused of killing Higashi to stop him from building up here."

"But where did you get such fine armor?" Okada asked.

Igarashi tossed his helmet to Okada. Okada put her hands out as if to stop a heavy object from hitting her but the helmet almost floated towards her. She caught it and peered at it in the dark. "It's paper!" she exclaimed.

"Igarashi made it for us," the second 'ghost' explained. "It's all paint and paper. The metal and cords are all painted. The swords are just painted wood. At a distance it is hard to tell the armor is not real."

"You killed my husband!" Higashi's wife screamed.

"No they didn't," I said firmly. "Your maid has already confessed and I've told you that my gaijin friend could look at the body and the scene and read the story of your crime as surely as if a scribe had written it. My friend even deduced that Igarashi made paper armor so the workmen would be scared away. He is the one who asked me to confront Igarashi to help us unravel the story of the murder. You believed in the ghosts of Shiraito Falls and tried to blame them but the loose threads of the crime have ensnared you. You murdered your husband and when Officer Suzuki arrives tomorrow you will pay for it."

Despite the blustering of Higashi's wife, Igarashi, the innkeeper, and Okada led her away. They assured me that she would be locked in a storage shed and guarded until morning. The maid, still wobbly from her fright at the ghosts, followed.

After they left, Sigerson built a fire and we sat by it watching the beautiful white threads of Shiraito Falls as they caught the light of the rising moon. When the crime was unsolved Sigerson-san had burned with the fire of enthusiasm. Now that the puzzle was solved he seemed to sink back into himself.

"Do you think we did the right thing, Sigerson-san?"

"What do you mean, Doctor?"

"In solving this crime. You said the world was better off with some people out of it and maybe Higashi was one such person."

"Maybe. But his wife is no better. Higashi was a brute but his wife is a murderer. Is one worse than the other?"

I left Sigerson-san's question unanswered. Instead I enjoyed the sight and sounds of the falls. Unfortunately, Sigerson-san didn't seem to find solace in the beauty of Shiraito in the moonlight. In fact, he looked positively bored. I thought about his request for cocaine that started this entire adventure.

"You know Sigerson-san, I was quite amazed that you were able to tell I had rowing as a hobby when I was in England the first time we met."

"I told you, Doctor, the calluses from rowing, although diminished by the passing years, are very distinctive."

"Do you know, Sigerson-san, that in Japan we row a boat quite differently than they do in England. In Japan we stand in the stern of the boat and use a single oar to propel the boat, much like the tail of a fish."

"Oh?"

"Yes. I imagine that would result in calluses very different than what you are used to seeing."

"I imagine so," Sigerson-san said, his interest piqued.

"Also, in Japan a carpenter would have very different calluses than a European carpenter. In Europe a saw cuts on the backstroke but in Japan we use saws that cut when they are pushed forward. That must result in a callus pattern different than what you are used to."

"I'm sure it would."

"To my knowledge no one has ever made a study of this. I'm sure that it would greatly help our Japanese police if a monograph could be written on the subject of identifying occupations by the callus pattern of the hands. If you would endeavor to write such a monograph I would be happy to translate it into Japanese and arrange with Officer Suzuki to have it distributed to police forces throughout the country."

Sigerson-san's face was not completely visible in the moonlight but I could tell from his body that he was like a racehorse straining at the starting gate.

"If you think that would be a useful addition to the police literature in Japan I would be interested in writing such a piece. You would have to help introduce me to people in various trades so I could study their hands and see the distinctive patterns that result from various occupations."

"When I am not engaged in my practice I would be very happy to do so, Sigerson-san."

"Good. If you don't mind we could start tomorrow after we return to your house."

"If I have no medical emergencies waiting for me I would be happy to start on such a study."

"Capital!"

In the darkness Sigerson-san probably could not see me smile but I felt there would be no requests for drugs to ward off boredom for quite some time to come.

The Case of the Broken Heart

The past is shadow.

The present can hide in that

shadow. Oh, my love.

"Sensei, you must do something about the gaijin guest!"

Hosokawa-san looked distressed to the point of tears. "What is the matter?" I asked.

"Those gaijin newspapers you got him…"

I had brought Sigerson-san an armful of old *London Times* newspapers from the Mampei thinking he might enjoy some news of Europe, even if it was not in a Norwegian newspaper. "What about them?"

"He's cut the paper into tiny pieces and piled them around his room. I tried to clean them up but he got upset. I don't know what he was saying but he stopped me from gathering all the paper bits up."

I was alarmed by this report from Hosokawa-san, although I know that it is easy to misinterpret what is going on if you can't speak each other's language. "I'll speak to Sigerson-san about it," I promised Hosokawa-san. I was going to add an admonition to her for still serving tubs of butter at every meal with Sigerson-san, a reference to the popular belief that gaijin always smell of butter, but from the strained look on her face I thought it was best to leave that until another time.

Later that afternoon Sigerson-san and I were playing a game of *Go*. They don't play Go in Europe.

Instead they prefer chess, which is a game very much like *shougi*, but with more ornate playing pieces. I started teaching Go to Sigerson-san to keep his mind occupied. Strangely, he was bored when he didn't have a "little diversion" to keep it occupied: In other words, a crime to solve.

I started instructing him in Go by giving Sigerson-san the usual nine-stone handicap. In a matter of a few days he had reduced the handicap to six stones and I thought he would soon be playing me with no handicap at all! As you might expect from his incredible eye for detail Sigerson-san was very good at the tactical infighting of Go but I was surprised he was also good at the strategic view of the whole board. With 361 possible positions to play on a Go board beginners usually lose sight of the strategic aspects as they grapple with the tactical, but not Sigerson-san. He grasped both the tactical and strategic concepts of this most difficult game, once again confirming the brilliance of his mind.

I placed a white stone down on the Go board with a pleasing click. Sigerson-san immediately placed a black stone down as if he had anticipated my move—most irritating when I was supposed to be the experienced player teaching him! Still, I told myself I was not concentrating on the game. I had other things on my mind.

"Sigerson-san?" I said.

"Yes, Doctor?"

I cleared my throat. I had been contemplating this for some time but was still very nervous about asking. "I've been thinking about your methodologies when you engage in your hobby of investigating crimes."

"Yes?"

"I understand the value of investigating a possible crime scene when it is fresh. Your ability to draw conclusions from the smallest physical details is amazing. However, I was wondering if any of your methods might prove useful when investigating a death that occurred years ago. It would be impossible to apply any direct observational methods so I was curious about how you go about examining the circumstances of such a death."

Sigerson-san paused, fixed his eyes on me, and said, "What is it about your wife's death that you find discomforting?"

I felt my face turn red with emotion. I had witnessed Sigerson-san's ability to make deductions before so I was not completely dumbfounded but I was embarrassed that my thoughts were so transparent. "How did you know I was making reference to the death of my late wife?" I asked.

"Normally you are a very observant and even-tempered man, Doctor; two valuable traits in both a physician and a companion. I know you have been watching my methods closely as your invaluable help in our little crime solving adventures has shown. However, tonight you have asked me about a topic we have not encountered, specifically the investigation of a death some years past. In addition, despite your efforts to remain casual, you have asked me this with a great deal of evident emotion. Whose death should evoke so much emotion even after years? From our first meeting I was able to deduce that your wife died a few years ago so it is a natural conclusion that you are interested in investigating the circumstances of your late wife's passing."

I sighed. When Sigerson-san explained his deductions it always seemed logical and simple but it would be difficult or impossible for the average person to draw the same conclusions given the same facts.

"I actually have no reason to be suspicious about her death, other than the fact she was a young woman in good health. It's just that I know so few details of her death. At the time I was on a business trip to Nagoya. My wife put me on the train to Nagoya the picture of health and three days later, when I reached Nagoya, there was a telegram asking me to return to Karuizawa because she had died."

"And you don't know the circumstances of her death?"

"I know the circumstances but not the details. At the time I was too shocked by her death to inquire too deeply. When she became ill she was attended to by Doctor Yamamoto, who used to be the senior physician in the little community of doctors here in Karuizawa. Dr. Yamamoto was a practitioner of traditional Chinese Medicine and tried to treat her with herbs but she was past the point where such treatment was effective." I shook my head sadly. "Unfortunately, Dr. Yamamoto himself has passed on since my wife's death and he is not here to answer the questions I have. I curse myself for not asking about her death before he passed but I was too brokenhearted to pursue the details until recently. I thought that perhaps your methods could help me find out more about the circumstances of her death."

"Did Dr. Yamamoto tell you exactly what she died of?"

"He said she died from eating bad food. He said her body was radically out of balance from something she ate and this caused her death. To give me an example of what he meant he mentioned that Tokugawa Ieyasu, the first Tokugawa Shogun, died from eating fish fried in sesame oil."

"Do you believe that?"

"I believe that Tokugawa Ieyasu died after eating but I don't believe it was caused by fried fish. I was taught the theories of Louis Pasteur as part of my studies and I'm aware that other causes of illness may be found in food."

"So you think your wife ate tainted food and that was the cause of her death?"

"I don't know. That is why I want to find out the details of her death and thought your methods might help me."

"Do you know anything about the events leading to your wife's death?"

"Just what Dr. Yamamoto and Hosokawa-san told me."

"So Mrs. Hosokawa was here?"

"Yes she was."

"Then perhaps we can start by interviewing her. When looking at something several years in the past it is unlikely that there is any direct observational evidence so we must rely on the imperfect memories of people. May I ask, Doctor, what you hope to discover?"

I cleared my throat. "I don't expect to discover anything except more details. I simply want to know more about her last hours on earth."

"I understand," Sigerson-san said sympathetically. He got directly to business. "Then let's start with Mrs. Hosokawa since she is in this household. Could you ask her to come in, Doctor, and translate for me as usual? I think we can put our Go game in abeyance."

I asked Hosokawa-san to join us in the parlor where we were playing. When she entered I could see she looked a bit apprehensive. I realized she might be concerned about her discussion with me about Sigerson-san's sloppy habits. Even though Hosokawa-san was given great leeway in my home she was still a servant and if she offended my guest it could be difficult for her. She would be reflecting badly on my household, not just her personal conduct. I immediately tried to put her at ease by saying, "We wanted to ask you about something that happened two years ago."

Her face relaxed a bit, then tensed up when she realized what I was referencing. "Are you talking about the death of the Lady, Sensei?" she asked.

"Yes. I know you told me about her illness when I returned from Nagoya but frankly at the time I was sick with grief. Now I want to learn a bit more about her death so I can satisfy my mind that I know about her last days."

Hosokawa-san looked a bit confused. "What else can I tell you, Sensei? I told you about the Lady's illness and my running to get Yamamoto-sensei."

When I translated this for Sigerson-san he said, "Please just ask Mrs. Hosokawa to try and remember what exactly happened before your wife died. Have her recount the events in chronological order. Inform her that details will be extremely important if we want to satisfy your need to understand how your wife died."

I translated this and added, "Please try your best, *ganbatte*, Hosokawa-san. I am now strong enough to know the details of my wife's death and knowing those details will comfort me."

She bowed. "Yes, Sensei."

"Now, on the day before your wife became ill can she tell me what your wife did?" Sigerson-san asked when I indicated both Hosokawa-san and I were ready to continue.

"That was the day after the Sensei left for Nagoya. I remember she went into town because she said she would do the shopping for me. I told her that was totally unnecessary but she said she would enjoy doing it."

"Did she go into town just to do shopping?" Sigerson-san asked.

"I don't think so because she was gone for a long time."

"Do you have any idea where she might have also gone?"

"No, I'm sorry, I don't."

"And when did Mrs. Watanabe get sick?"

"That very night. It was awful. I wanted to get a doctor right away and she said it must just be something she ate. The next morning when I went to wake her she was unconscious and I ran to get Dr. Yamamoto. He came right away but by that evening the Lady had passed." As I translated this I could see tears in Hosokawa-san's eyes. I suddenly realized there were tears in my eyes, too.

"Can you think of anything that might help us discover where Mrs. Watanabe went that day?" Sigerson-san said. He was far too perceptive to not see the show of emotion from Hosokawa-san and myself but he acted as though he did not notice. In this, he was acting very much like a Japanese, pretending not to see what is clearly visible to avoid embarrassing us.

"No, I can't." Then Hosokawa-san got a look on her face as if she remembered something. "I know she brought some fresh local mushrooms that she purchased at a store by the train station. She said the local mushrooms were especially delicious."

"Did she eat the mushrooms she bought for dinner?"

"Yes, but I ate them too. Dr. Yamamoto did not think the mushrooms caused her death."

"How did you prepare the mushrooms?"

"I cut them in strips and cooked them in a broth of *shouyu* and sake. The Lady was correct and they were especially delicious. I actually ate more of them than she did."

"Is there anything else you can tell us?"

"Just that the Lady became sick that night and by the next evening she had passed. It was all so sudden." Hosokawa-san broke down completely at this, the tears flowing like water. Even Sigerson-san, with all his scientific detachment could not ignore this display. He leaned forward and gently touched her arm. She seemed startled by this gesture and looked at him in surprise. "Please tell Mrs. Hosokawa that I understand she lost more than a mistress," Sigerson-san said. "I know she lost a friend."

I admit it took me a few seconds to summon up the composure to translate this because I was close to breaking down in tears again, something I thought was over with the first few months after my wife's death. But I suppose my emotions were still raw just below the skin of conventional calm. We Japanese consider ourselves an emotional people which is why we value self-control and composure. But we Japanese men almost never tell our wives we love them. We just expect them to know that from the things we do for them. In truth, Japanese men are usually embarrassed by such displays of affection, except to our children. I now wish I had summoned the courage to tell my late wife that I loved her every one of the short days we were together.

After I was able to translate Sigerson-san's statement to Hosokawa-san she was able to regain her harmony. Then she bowed to Sigerson-san and gave him the first genuinely kind look since he had joined my household.

"That's all the questions I have now," Sigerson-san said with his usual brisk English manner. But the kind look in his eyes did not go away.

When Hosokawa-san left the room I turned to Sigerson-san and he asked me, "From what you know about your wife's illness, could it have been caused by the mushrooms?"

"Her symptoms would fit some kinds of mushroom poisoning. But I can see why Dr. Yamamoto did not draw that diagnosis. It is unlikely that mushrooms would poison my wife and not affect Hosokawa-san, who also ate them with her. After all, Hosokawa-san said she cut the mushrooms into strips so it would be unlikely that my wife would eat a particular poison mushroom but not Hosokawa-san. Dr. Yamamoto thought something my wife ate caused her illness, but he specifically rejected the mushrooms."

Sigerson-san raised a finger in admonition. "At this stage, Doctor, it is very important not to accept fully the ideas of others. Currently there is no direct evidence or deductions that will give us details about your wife's passing. We are forced to rely on the memories of people, but memory can be an ephemeral thing. Facts don't change but human memory of facts does. That is why my methods depend on direct observation and logic. One thing we must avoid at all hazards is accepting the conclusions of others, absent convincing evidence that these conclusions are accurate."

I nodded my understanding. "So what is our next step?" I asked.

"I think we should walk into town and find the store Mrs. Hosokawa mentioned. Your wife bought mushrooms at a store near the station and we should seek out this establishment. In a situation like this we must follow the thread of memory, no matter how thin it may be."

We made our way down to the station. Many shops were clustered around the station and we went into several of them until we found one that had fresh local mushrooms for sale. The mushrooms sat in a flat basket and looked delicious. The owner of the shop came up to us with an obsequious smile. Gaijin were common in the town of Karuizawa so he didn't give Sigerson-san a second glance.

"Can I help you gentlemen?" he said.

"Your mushrooms look good," I answered.

"Ah, yes. They're local mushrooms and, if I may say so, they are the best you will find in Karuizawa."

"Why do you say that?"

"Because I have a little secret about mushrooms."

"Which is?"

"To get the best mushrooms you must find the best mushroom hunter. My mushrooms come from the best mushroom hunter in all of Karuizawa."

"Who is this person?"

"Her name is Takada-san."

I was a bit startled by this name so I asked, "Is she a woman in her forties, with a pinched face and a very… ah, aggressive personality?"

The shop owner grinned but this time it was a rueful grin. "I see you know the lady. That is a good description of her," he said.

I filled in Sigerson-san about this development including the fact that Takada-san was a patient of mine. If this was of interest to him he didn't immediately show it but he was often good at keeping an inscrutable face. "Do you think he might remember your wife buying mushrooms two years ago?" he asked.

I posed that question to the shopkeeper but he couldn't remember a sale from that long ago. Sigerson-san and I left the shop and I asked him, "What should we do next?"

"Visit Mrs. Takada."

"Why?"

"Because if the trail ends with Mrs. Takada then we have run out of avenues to explore."

By now I had developed an inexhaustible faith in Sigerson-san's ability to unravel mysteries so it was a sobering admission that details about my wife's passing may end at Takada-san's door.

We walked back to my office so I could check my records to see where Takada-san lived. As we walked I told Sigerson-san about Takada-san's insistence in trying to arrange a marriage meeting, a miai, with her daughter.

"When did she start that?" he asked.

"About two and a half years ago, soon after I came to Karuizawa," I answered.

"So she started before your wife passed?"

"Yes, but she stopped as soon as I told her I was already married."

"And how long did she wait after your wife died before she started pestering you again."

"Not long enough. Frankly, her insistence at trying to arrange a marriage meeting for me is one thing that I can't stand about Takada-san."

"But you still treat her as a physician."

"If a physician only treated patients he liked most doctors would have a very small practice."

Sigerson-san gave me one of his fleeting smiles. Making a little joke made me feel better. Trying to retrace the last steps of my wife was very taxing on me, but it was something I felt I had to do.

At my home I checked Takada-san's records to see where she lived. We set off for the Takada house, which was a short walk away from my house. When we got to the Takada house I saw that it was a small but respectable home. It was not ostentatious and did not reflect wealth but it did not represent someone living in poverty, either.

I went to the front door and politely called out, "Sumimasen!" From inside the small house I heard a "Hai, hai!" and I stepped back from the door respectfully. The door slid open and Takada-san stuck her head out. She saw me and a whole range of emotions passed across her face. First was shock, then surprise, then pleasure and finally, and most unattractively, triumph. I'm sure Takada-san thought that all her nagging about her daughter had motivated me to visit.

"Sensei!" she exclaimed. "Please come in, come in! Please ask your gaijin friend to come in, too. I am most happy to see you, although Naomi-chan is not home at this moment." From the smirk on Takada-san's face I believe this last remark was to reassure me I could talk about marriage freely, if I wished to. I, of course, did not wish to.

We entered the house and sat in the small living room. Sigerson-san took off his shoes at the entryway and sat on a zabuton cushion as I sat next to him. Takada-san bustled off.

"Where is she going?" Sigerson-san asked.

"To get us tea and a snack," I answered.

"Is that necessary?" Sigerson-san responded.

"Yes," I said. "Even though Takada-san is not the most refined person there are certain proprieties that must be observed when visitors call. Refreshments are one of them."

Sigerson-san fidgeted next to me but he made no further comments. He was a man who preferred going directly to the point, much like an impatient child. When he was not working on a puzzle he could be incredibly indolent. But when he was in the midst of a task I have never seen a person more focused and driven.

Takada-san returned with a tray containing three teacups and three small dishes. On each dish was a small pile of cooked mushrooms, garnished with a tiny pinch of baby radish greens.

I took a mushroom and tasted it. It was delicious, with a light shouyu and *miso* taste that enhanced the natural earthiness of the mushroom. Sigerson-san, who was still a bit clumsy using hashi, chopsticks, took a bit longer to get a mushroom in his mouth but, once he did, I could tell he was pleased with the taste.

"These mushrooms are delicious," I proclaimed.

"Thank you," Takada-san responded, "but they're really nothing special. Just local mushrooms I gathered myself."

"I was told you sell mushrooms to one of the local stores."

Takada-san seemed surprised I knew this. "Yes. I gather them here in the mountains. My late husband left us comfortable enough but after Naomi-chan and I moved here I discovered there were abundant local mushrooms if you know where to find them. I use the extra money I earn gathering mushrooms to pay for lessons for Naomi-chan."

"Lessons?"

"Yes. Things like *kadou* and *chadou*—traditional arts that the wife of a fine gentleman will need."

This was a little too blatant so I changed the subject. "You mentioned you moved here. Does that mean you lived somewhere else before Karuizawa?"

"Yes. My husband and I used to live in Matsui. He died young and soon after he died I decided to move to Karuizawa. I wanted a change of atmosphere and a chance for Naomi-chan to meet suitable people. Compared to Matsui, Karuizawa has quite a cosmopolitan atmosphere because of the many Westerners and Japanese who live or visit here."

"You have devoted much of your life to your daughter."

"She is my great hope in life. She will do the things I was not able to do."

The fervent intensity of her statement shocked and surprised me. I began to understand that Takada-san's promotion of her daughter as a marriage partner went beyond gauche insistence but instead bordered on fanaticism. To give myself a chance to think about what Takada-san said I took the time to translate our conversation for Sigerson-san. He seemed satisfied with what I was doing so I continued my conversation with Takada-san.

"Takada-san, the reason I disturbed you today was because I am trying to trace the steps of my late wife. I am interested in knowing more about her last hours on earth."

Takada-san looked surprised, which is what I expected, but her next words made it my turn to be surprised. "I don't think there is anything I can help you with on that topic, Sensei. Besides, I have found it best to forget the past and not dwell on it. After all, *shikata ga nai, ne*? It can't be helped, right?"

Her presumptuous words didn't bother me: this, after all, was the kind of statement I had come to expect from Takada-san. Instead it was her manner of speaking that caught my attention. She spoke slowly and carefully as if choosing every word with extreme caution. This was not because of any particular sensitivity to the topic, I believe. I think it was because of fear.

Her way of saying this was so singular that I saw Sigerson-san take notice even though he could not, of course, understand her.

"So you know nothing of my wife's last day? Hosokawa-san told me that she went into town and I thought perhaps she might have visited you for some reason."

"Oh, no, Sensei. I met your wife a few times but she never honored me with a visit to my humble home."

When she said that I knew she was lying. The question was why she was lying.

During my association with Sigerson-san I had come into contact with more crime and death than I ever had before. Now frightening and ugly thoughts entered my head. I wanted desperately to discuss these thoughts with Sigerson-san so I finished the conversation with Takada-san as soon as possible. As Sigerson-san and I walked back to my house I told him of my fears.

"You have studied my methods rather closely, Doctor," Sigerson-san said. "Based on what you have told me your deductions may be correct, but in fact there is another possibility and you must keep your mind open until evidence appears that lets you understand what the truth is."

"But what new evidence can appear at this late date?" I asked. "My wife died two years ago and you said how difficult it is to investigate a situation that is so old."

"That is why we must conduct a rather simple experiment, Doctor. I assure you that once the experiment is over we will know the truth of things."

A few days later Sigerson-san and I were climbing up the slope of one of the mountains that surround Karuizawa. The air was a bit cold but very crisp and refreshing. "Sensei! Sensei!" The familiar voice of Takada-san reached us as Sigerson-san and I made our way around a curve in the path.

Takada-san and Naomi-chan were waiting for us by the side of the path. Takada-san was wearing sensible work clothes, a short jacket and *monpe*, the farmer's work pants. Naomi-chan, however, was wearing a pink kimono. In another setting the kimono might have been appropriate and even charming but to go mushroom hunting it was clearly ridiculous attire. Naomi-chan seemed to realize this because she hung her face in embarrassment. It was obvious that the kimono was Takada-san's idea, I suppose to make Naomi-chan more attractive to me.

Takada-san was exuberant and smiling broadly as she bowed to greet Sigerson-san and me. Hosokawa-san, who had delivered my note to Takada-san asking her to teach Sigerson-san and myself how to hunt mushrooms, had told me Takada-san seemed ecstatic when she read my request. Takada-san readily agreed and promptly set a time and place.

"Please go with Naomi-chan, Sensei," Takada-san suggested. "I will be happy to take the gaijin-sama with me."

"Do you speak English, Takada-san?"

"No, I do not, Sensei."

"Then it might be best for you to pair up with Naomi-chan while I stay with Sigerson-san. You can give us instructions and I can translate. After all, it is Sigerson-san that has an intense interest in how you identify and pick local Japanese mushrooms."

Takada-san was clearly unhappy with this arrangement but she could not invent a good reason to throw Naomi-chan and me together so she grudgingly accepted the arrangement. Taking woven baskets that Takada-san had brought, the four of us entered the woods.

"You must look closely for local mushrooms, especially where wood has piled naturally," Takada-san began her lesson. "Look especially on the down-slope base of trees, looking for a patch of brown color. Sometimes there will be a cluster of mushrooms and sometimes just a single mushroom."

As we went deeper in the forest Naomi-chan had increasing problems keeping up. Moving through a wooded and brush-filled mountainside was difficult enough in trousers; it was almost impossible in a kimono. Even Takada-san saw the absurdity of this outfit on a mushroom hunt and she sent Naomi-chan back to the road to wait for us.

Takada-san saw the first mushrooms and pounced on them greedily. She really was good at spotting mushrooms. Her eyes were keen and she was always looking in the various folds and hidden spots formed by fallen trees and the natural contours of the land to spot mushrooms.

Soon Sigerson-san and I found a few mushrooms but nothing like Takada-san's filling basket. Near a large pine tree I saw a mushroom growing at the base of a *sugi* tree. I bent to pick it when I heard Takada-san saying, "Sensei! Don't pick that mushroom!"

I looked over and saw Takada-san almost ten meters away from me. She was running towards me and waving her hands, almost slipping on the steep slope of the mountain. When she reached me she said, "That is a poison mushroom, Sensei! Be careful. Don't pick it!"

I looked at her for several moments, digesting the full import of what she was telling me. "You could tell it was poison from where you were standing?" I asked.

"Yes." She pointed to the mushroom. "See the cap of the mushroom is almost a brownish-black. A local mushroom that is edible has a brown cap, not so dark. It's a common mistake to confuse the poisonous and non-poisonous mushrooms if you are not experienced."

"But someone as experienced as you can tell the difference from almost ten meters away."

Takada-san nodded. "Of course. I have been picking mushrooms all of my life. I can easily tell the safe mushrooms from the dangerous ones."

"I thought that might be the case," I said, "but I just wanted to test you. I knew this mushroom was poisonous. I was about to pick it exactly for that reason." Takada-san gave me a surprised look. "I thought we would have to wait until we sorted through the mushrooms we collected to test you but you've shown your ability to identify a poisonous mushroom even from a distance."

"I don't understand, Sensei," Takada-san said.

"You may not understand but now I understand," I answered. "I understand you were lying when you said my wife never visited you at your home. The first time I met Naomi-chan she said how sorry she was at my loss. She mentioned she had met my wife when she stopped at your house and she thought my wife was nice. Why would you lie to me about my wife being at your house?"

Takada-san said nothing.

"I also understand how my wife knew the local mushrooms were delicious two years ago. You served her mushrooms when she visited you."

I waited for Takada-san's denial, but she hesitated a moment. I could see her answer would be in the same deliberat fashion she used when Sigerson-san and I visited her. A fashion of speaking designed not to incriminate her. I didn't give her a chance to start.

"I also understand that what Sigerson-san told me was right," I continued. "He said there are some monsters in life that will kill humans as other people will kill flies. You are such a person. Your ambition for your daughter knows no bounds, even the bounds of civilization and decency. I don't think your daughter shares your ambition but you decided that she should marry a doctor. In fact, you decided she should marry me. The fact I already had a wife was of little consequence to you. You invited my wife to visit you and you poisoned her. You killed her simply to remove an obstacle to your ambitions."

"But Sensei…"

"Shut up!" The rudeness of my shout struck Takada-san like a slap. I thought I was being calm during this discourse but I noticed that my friend Sigerson-san had his hand on my arm to restrain me. I realized that, given the slightest provocation, I could kill Takada-san on the spot. How close we are to the beast within.

"Sigerson-san said that it was possible the poisoning might be an accident. He said you might be afraid to admit my wife had eaten the poison mushrooms at your house because you knew you would be blamed for her death. He said her death might not necessarily be murder.

That is why we conducted this little experiment with you. You have passed the test of your ability to identify a poison mushroom with highest marks. You have also branded yourself a murderer. It was no mistake that you fed a poison mushroom to my wife. Sigerson-san told me that if you are a murderer, the chances are that a person like you will have killed in the past. I am going to write the police chief in Matsui and ask him to investigate the circumstances of your husband's death. If he died with symptoms like my wife's you are going to have a hard time explaining how an expert mushroom hunter such as yourself has killed people."

I didn't trust myself to say more to Takada-san and turned to leave, dropping my basket of mushrooms on the ground. Sigerson-san followed me back towards the path, his long legs allowing him to keep up with my rapid pace.

At the path Naomi-chan was surprised to see us, especially since her mother was not with us. "Is there something wrong, Sensei?" she asked.

I simply bowed to her and started walking down the path. I had no animosity towards Naomi-chan for her mother's monstrous behavior. From my observations Naomi-chan had suffered from her mother's ambitions and pretentions. I just didn't want to tell Naomi-chan that her mother was a murderer. At least not at that moment.

Sigerson-san walked with me in silence until I felt able to tell him about my conversation with Takada-san. He remained silent during my recitation and afterwards. It's dangerous to project Japanese sensibilities onto gaijin but I felt that Sigerson-san understood that no words were necessary in this situation.

I wrote the letter to the police chief of Matsui as soon as we reached my house. Then Sigerson-san suggested that we resume our game of Go. He didn't talk about Takada-san and I felt he suggested the game of Go because he thought it would take my mind off the terrible implications of Takada-san poisoning my wife.

We played most of the game in silence. It was very Japanese of us to ignore the unpleasant specter that hovered around us. At the end of the game I said, "I will soon have to reduce your handicap to five stones."

"But you beat me."

"But not by much. Your progress in Go is remarkable. I think if you stay in Japan you will soon become a *shodan*, the first step on the road to becoming a professional Go player. It shows what an incredible mind you have."

"Thank you, Doctor. By the way, I have to thank you for the chest of drawers you gave me. It is very suitable for organizing the newspaper clippings I like to save."

I had purchased a *kodansu* chest of drawers for Sigerson-san. I learned, after Hosokawa-san's protest about the mess, that Sigerson-san was clipping articles about murders, kidnappings, embezzlements, and other crimes and odd happenings from the English papers and saving them for some reason. I didn't ask him the reason but I did buy him the small chest of drawers so he would have a way of organizing and keeping these clippings without Hosokawa-san objecting to the clutter.

I was debating the wisdom of telling him about Hosokawa-san's objection to any mess when the good woman came into the house after doing her daily shopping in town.

"Did you hear, Sensei?" she said to me. "The whole town is talking about it!"

"Did I hear what?"

"Takada-san hanged herself! No one knows why."

I thought about the letter sitting on my desk and I knew perfectly well why she committed suicide. I told Sigerson-san the news. He seemed surprised. In England I've heard of cases where members of the military or the upper class commit suicide to avoid a scandal but I think it is uncommon for a criminal to commit suicide, to atone for the crime, unlike here in Japan.

"So, it's over," Sigerson-san said. It was the first time he had referred to Takada-san murdering my wife since the forest.

I was about to say that I wasn't sure that it would ever be over, at least for me, when Hosokawa-san interrupted us again.

"I'm sorry to disturb you, Sensei, but this was delivered for you. I brought it back from town with me. It's a note from Takada-san."

I looked at the formal folded envelope Hosokawa-san gave me. On the front was my name, written in a thin and untutored hand. I thanked Hosokawa-san and dismissed her even though it was obvious she wanted to stay and see what the note said.

"What is that?" Sigerson-san asked.

"A note from Takada-san." I put the note in my pocket.

Sigerson-san, even though he had superb self-control, couldn't help himself. He asked, "Aren't you going to read it?"

"No," I said. "I think not. It could be a note of apology for the murder of my wife, but knowing Takada-san it's just as likely to be a note that claims she committed suicide to protest an unjust accusation. In either case I don't care what she had to say. Nothing she can write and nothing she can do, including taking her own life, will bring my beloved wife back. I know from following your methods we have gotten to the truth about my wife's death." And then, I am not ashamed to say, I sat in front of an uncomfortable Sigerson-san and cried.

Author's End Notes

Furutani is an unusual name.

I expect most people to find it a little unusual in the United States but it's even unusual in Japan. If a Japanese looks at the kanji characters that make up my name, he or she will probably think it's "Furuya." Furuya is not an uncommon name but kanji characters can have alternative readings and my family pronounces the second character in our name as "tani," not "ya." Thus we're Furutani (which means "old valley" or "ancient valley"). You don't find many Furutanis in Japan unless you happen to travel to Yamaguchi Prefecture and Oshima in the Seto Sea, where my family originally comes from.

Because our name is unusual I have a working theory that almost every Furutani is related in some way. This may not actually be true but it's a good ice breaker on the rare occasions that I've come across another Furutani.

While my wife and I were living in Japan our friend Naoko-san said to us that she had come across another Furutani. When she told me that my ears pricked up because I had met only one other Furutani in Japan, despite years of living there. Naoko-san is the granddaughter of an Akutagawa Prize winning novelist and she's one of those sweet people who seem to make friends easily. She told me that she was at her family's cabin in Karuizawa and wandered into town to explore portions she wasn't familiar with. There she came across an old curio shop of truly ancient vintage.

The obaasan who owned the shop turned out to be a Furutani. Naoko-san has a way of connecting with people and within a few minutes they were apparently chattering away like old friends. During the course of this conversation Naoko-san mentioned she had an American friend who was also named Furutani. When Naoko-san said

I was a writer, the obaasan became very excited and begged Naoko-san to ask me to visit Karuizawa and to make time to meet her when I did.

I've been to Karuizawa and although I enjoyed my visit I usually like to explore places in Japan I've never been to before. Still, Karuizawa is only a short bullet-train ride from Tokyo and Naoko-san was very insistent that I should see this Furutani who lived in Karuizawa so I boarded the *Shinkansen* at Tokyo Station and shortly found myself out of the bustle of Tokyo and in the clean mountain air of Karuizawa.

Following Naoko-san's instructions it was fairly easy to find the curiosity shop (or as easy as finding anything in Japan can be—the building numbers are not sequential and many roads are not named so even the Japanese get lost frequently). The shop is located in an old-fashioned Japanese house. Most Western tourists would not realize it was a store.

In an old-fashioned store in Japan the goods are usually brought to you as you sit and sip tea. There are few, if any, display cases of merchandise. I initially peeked in through the open door and I saw a shaded tatami room with a few old scrolls hanging from the wall. There was a sign in front of the house but I don't read Japanese and I was confused about the nature of the establishment. I thought I was intruding on a private residence and I was about to retreat in embarrassment and confusion when a tiny old woman, who was sitting in a corner of the room unnoticed, looked up at me and spoke.

"*Ohayou gozaimasu!*" she said cheerfully. Good manners demanded that I respond. "Ohayou gozaimasu," good morning, I said. She greeted my pitiful Japanese with a bright smile that lit up her wrinkled face.

The old obaasan who ran this store took a fancy to me for some reason. My Japanese is very poor but we managed to communicate with a combination of broken Japanese, a few words of English, and pantomime. When I mentioned Naoko-san's name the obaasan's face lit up. When she found out I was Furutani, the writer Naoko-san had mentioned, she was beyond excitement.

She immediately gave me the box with the precious notebooks of Doctor Junichi Watanabe.

Because of the devastation caused by World War II it is difficult to piece together more about Dr. Watanabe's life from the official records. I don't know when he was born or when he died, although the notebooks tell us he was living and practicing medicine in Karuizawa in 1892-1893 when Sherlock Holmes apparently slipped into Japan.

We can also tell that Dr. Watanabe was a man of his time. He was cosmopolitan from his visit to England and apparently had extremely good English language skills but he also was proud of his samurai heritage. For instance, nowhere in the first notebook does he add the honorific "san" to the name of a shopkeeper. Until the end of feudalism merchants were on the lowest rung of society's ladder and Watanabe apparently had a lingering prejudice in this area. A notable exception to his sense of social class was his reference to his housekeeper as "Hosokawa-san." This was a marked sign of the affection he had for this lady.

When dealing with a foreigner like Holmes Watanabe still retained some very Japanese attitudes. Watanabe had an appreciation of Holmes's brilliance and skills but he also often judged Holmes by Japanese norms and often found him wanting. Of course, even a partisan English observer like Dr. John Watson sometimes found the many Holmes eccentricities worth recording.

Regardless, it is plain that Watanabe considered Holmes a friend who injected a great deal of excitement and novelty into his life.

I found a book in English printed in Japan in 1911 titled *An Invitation to Renga*. A Renga is a collaborative linked verse, starting with what we now call a haiku. The idea was another poet will take the starting haiku and add to it. The renga book was written by Junichi Watanabe. There is no way to know for certain if this is the same Junichi Watanabe who wrote the notebooks but there is an excellent chance they are one and the same. In any case, I've used haiku found in this book to introduce each of the stories.

I've mentioned that the notebooks are in the form of notes. The dialogue is faithfully recorded in detail but the doctor's observations are abbreviated. For instance, an early passage in the first notebook literally reads (Japanese words, in kanji or hiragana, are italicized):

"In my *experience strangest henna gaijin most brilliant* Norwegian Sigerson-san *perceptive blind—sensitive numb—refined boorish—brilliant* hopelessly *ignorant about Japan* sharing many adventures—*he* cipher last *time* saw him as the first *truly a henna gaijin*."

I've rewritten this as:

"In my experience, the strangest henna gaijin I've met was also the most brilliant. He was a Norwegian called Sigerson-san. He was by turns perceptive and blind, sensitive and numb, refined and boorish, brilliant and hopelessly ignorant, at least about Japan. Despite sharing many adventures with this man, he was almost as much a cipher the last time I saw him as the first time I met him: Truly a henna gaijin."

I hope Dr. Watanabe forgives me if my interpretation of his notes is not what he intended.

Having found the notebooks of Junichi Watanabe another little mystery was solved for me, by the way. The first time I went to Karuizawa, long before I knew about the notebooks and the Holmes visit to Japan, I went to a park in Karuizawa near the high school. You can go there yourself if you ever happen to visit Karuizawa. At the park I was puzzled to see the statue of a man. The figure is staring off into the mountains that surround Karuizawa, dressed in a familiar cape and hat. The statue is of Sherlock Holmes.

DALE FURUTANI is the first Asian-American to win major mystery writing awards and his books have appeared on numerous bestseller lists. He has spoken at the US Library of Congress, the Japanese-American National Museum, The Pacific Asia Museum, and numerous conferences. The City of Los Angeles named him as one of its "Forty Faces of Diversity" and *Publisher's Weekly* called him "a master craftsman." He has lived in Japan and traveled there extensively. He now lives with his wife in the Pacific Northwest.

Website: DALEFURUTANI.COM

ALSO BY DALE FURUTANI

Death in Little Tokyo
The Toyotomi Blades
Death at the Crossroads
Jade Palace Vendetta
Kill the Shogun
The Curious Adventures of Sherlock Holmes in Japan

"Dead Time," *Shaken: Stories for Japan* (anthology written to aid victims of the Great East Japan Earthquake and tsumami)
"Extreme Prejudice," *Murder on Sunset Boulevard* (anthology to benefit the L.A. chapter of Sisters in Crime)

Back cover author watercolor portrait by

Shannon Perry

Book Jacket illustration by

Vincent Dutreuil

Made in the USA
Monee, IL
08 November 2019